THE SWAN KING

A Mystery

Kevin Greene

To the untold number of writers, artists, editors
and publishers who have now and in the past
contributed to the most underrated art form known to
man

and

to my little guy William:
The best thing I have ever done.

I own nothing. It is only through the grace and kindness of the many copyright holders of the many comics mentioned here that I am allowed to publish this. I thank them for permitting me this honor of showing my love of the medium in these words.

THE SWAN KING

1

I was watching a marathon of *Doctor Who*, or, more accurately, a marathon of *Doctor Who* was watching me one Sunday night when my cell phone rang. I sat up on the couch in my dark living room lit only by the TV, blinked a few times and reached for my phone, almost knocking over a cold, half empty bowl of Beef Lo Mein. My cat Thor, who was lying on my lap, gave me annoyed and climbed off. Bachelor life. I slapped the phone around a little on the coffee table, finally got a hold of it and answered.

"Hello?"

"Hello," said an attractive sounding voice. "Is this William Farrar?

I sat up more and shook some more cobwebs away. On

TV, The Doctor was being dragged into the Pandorica by all of his enemies in a last ditch effort to imprison him forever. There were days where I could almost relate. Glancing at the cable box, I saw it was 9:52. The Mets were playing the Dodgers on *Sunday Night Baseball* on ESPN. It was well into the game already. Man, I had really dozed off.

"Um… yes it is. How can I help you?"

"Mr. Farrar, my name is Jessica Chandler. I'm calling on behalf of my father. He heard that you are very good at finding original comic pages and he's very interested in finding a particular one."

I reached over and turned the floor lamp on next to the couch. I don't know why; it wouldn't help the conversation any. Thor squinted, jumped down from the couch and walked out. Cats.

I rubbed my face and tried to not make any sounds as I stretched my free arm and legs out. I'm not sure how successful I was. "Ok. What is he looking for?"

"Well, I would rather he discuss it with you personally. Would you be able to come out to South Orange, New Jersey? Are you familiar with it?"

I had a buddy back in the day that went to Seton Hall so I did my fair share of hanging out in that area. I hadn't been back in awhile but I didn't mind returning. There was a comic store on South Orange Avenue that I could pop in on, too. It was almost impossible for me to not drop into a comic book store if I were near one. Occupational hazard.

"Yes, I've been," I said. "I can drive out. When did you want me to come by?"

"Oh, you drive," she said, surprised. "I didn't expect you to have a car. I thought most people in the city got around by train."

"I still do. But there have been more and more times where I need a car so I caved in and bought one. Most of my time driving it is switching which side of the street it's parked on."

She laughed politely. "I imagine. Well, the address is 394 North Ridgewood Road. Will you need directions?"

"No, I'm good. Around 11 tomorrow ok?"

She agreed and we hung up. 394 North Ridgewood Road. I texted myself the address, got the remote and turned from BBC America to ESPN. The Mets were down 2-0 in the 7th inning. I went to the kitchen, got a Corona and dropped back on the couch. Hmm. I wondered what page this guy was looking for. If he lived around where I thought he did, he was probably doing ok money-wise. There was no telling what he wanted or how much he was willing to put out for it. Interesting. I had just found a Neal Adams Batman page for a guy and brokered the deal between he and the seller that netted me a good bit of cash. Maybe this could be just as good. Definitely worth driving to Jersey for. On TV, Matt Kemp hit a homerun and the Mets were down 3-0. I finished my beer and at some point, with Thor back on my lap and the floor lamp back off, fell back asleep.

The next morning I got up and put on my usual spring attire; Dark jeans, denim shirt with a long sleeve tee underneath, a pair of Nikes and my ever-present blue on blue Mets hat. Fashionable. I left a little later than I wanted to but it was after rush hour and I was going against traffic, which usually flows from Jersey to New York in the mornings. I decided to avoid the Verrazano/Goethals bridge way through Staten Island and went the Manhattan way. I left my apartment on East 19th St. in Brooklyn and drove up Flatbush Avenue in my prize possession black Call of Duty Jeep Wrangler, heading towards the Manhattan Bridge. On ESPN radio Mike and Mike were discussing the NFL draft, segueing somehow into an argument about using your cellphone in the bathroom. It was a beautiful spring morning, still a little cool but with the temperature easing up into the high sixties. There wasn't a cloud in the brilliant blue sky and I had my windows down as I drove across the bridge, glancing at the new Freedom Tower where the WTC used to be. The bridge led over the East River and the FDR, still a little heavy with traffic, through the granite arch and colonnade at its mouth and then onto Canal Street, right at Chinatown. I stayed on Canal and made my way across to the west side. This was one of the slowest parts of the trip. Traffic was always heavy and there were a lot of people out, strolling, looking in the just opened shops, maybe heading to work late. Mike and Mike gave way to Colin Cowherd, who opened his show with a Carmelo Anthony rant, which I disagreed with. Eventually I turned onto the entrance of the Holland Tunnel to Jersey and drove in, raising my windows. Nothing like a mouthful of car, truck and bus exhaust to ruin a perfectly good morning.

I emerged on the 1 and 9 on the Jersey side, which slices through Jersey City, snaking it's way on elevated and non elevated roadways, through endless construction until it becomes the Pulaski Skyway, the notorious steel monolith that looms over a good portion of that area and memorably got blown up in the Spielberg/Cruise version of *War Of The Worlds.* Mercifully, I got off just before then, getting on Route 7, past more construction and then around two huge, seemingly useless loops before crossing the old Wittpenn draw bridge towards Kearny. It's such a convoluted way to go. Imagine going to the bathroom in your house by walking out your front door, climbing up a ladder leaning against the house, scrambling across the roof and down through the bathroom window. It seemed just about that sensible.

But it wasn't over yet, though it did get a little simpler. I headed to Route 280, which took me past Kearny and Harrison and through Newark. It usually bogs down there but again I lucked out and soon enough I was through the other Oranges before exiting into West Orange right on the South Orange border. Not too long after that I was driving up North Ridgewood Road and noticing the change from smaller, tightly spaced homes to larger, fancier ones on bigger lots. I always loved these houses, especially further up the hill towards the reservation at the crest of the incline, where there were woods and small streams. If I had the money, I would definitely buy a home in this area. That being a very big "if".

I got to 394 North Ridgewood Road and realized that "if" was even bigger. The house sat on private grounds behind a huge black wrought iron gate that no doubt circled the property. At the entry gate and drive there was a small sentry house on the outside and a metal call box on the driver's side. I couldn't even see the house from where I was. Big trees sat in a row behind the gate, their branches casting a nice shade over the drive. I pulled up to the box and looked at my watch. 10:46. I hate being too early but it might just take me fourteen minutes to find where the hell I was going. I pressed the little button on the box and waited. Off in the distance I could hear lawnmowers, more than one, no doubt meaning landscapers. Probably not too many people around here did the yard work themselves. A series of sprinklers were doing their job at the house across the street, gently spraying a massive front lawn. A jogger went by, a redhead with a white cap, magenta top and black leggings. She ran easily and looked pretty good doing it. Tough neighborhood.

The silver box let out a split second of static and then Jessica Chandler's voice came through clearly. "Yes?"

"Hello Jessica, it's William Farrar. I'm a little early."

"Oh, hello!" she said. "That's fine! Come up the drive and park near the other cars. I'll meet you at the front door."

The gate started moving soundlessly open. Somebody probably came out and oiled it twice a month for it to be that quiet. Maybe a special rolling-gate oiling robot did it. In this neighborhood I wouldn't be the least bit surprised.

I drove through the gate and up the drive and finally the house became visible. It was like something out of a British television show. *South Orange Abbey*. It was all muted red brick and stone with a sloping slate roof and large windows that had what seemed like a million panes in each. Ivy crept up the left side of the house, covering at least two thirds of the height, which was pretty impressive because the house was very tall. Out front there were neatly manicured hedges in stone pots, standing high over an explosion of multi-colored flowers and plants. The whole house was surrounded by a beige gravel walkway and drive. The place was huge. I half expected Alfred to come out and tell me that Master Bruce was indisposed at the moment.

There was a garage to the right of the house that you would only be disappointed in if you had more than eight cars. There was a sleek, black Audi R8 sitting in front of one of the open doors and next to it there was a short, muscled guy in a tight black tee shirt and shorts squirting water from a hose onto an absolutely stunning silver Bentley Mulsanne. Just washing that car was a privilege. I pulled up about twenty feet away and got out, leaving my Mets hat in the Jeep. Chandler was probably a Yankee fan and all I needed was for him to insult the Mets. Punching a prospective client was never good.

Short muscle guy stopped what he was doing and stared at me. He probably wasn't that short but being that wide made him look it. He definitely had the build and stance of a serious workout nut: The overdeveloped trapezius, the huge biceps, the insanely large calf muscles. He eyed me up and down, kind of like he was sizing me up. Were we supposed to fight? Was this to be a "Find my comic art then take on my driver in a steel cage death match" sort of visit? I really needed to get more info before I made these trips.

I gave SMG a head nod and a "Howyoudoin'?" but he just stared for a few more seconds and then resumed washing the car. Yup. Death match.

I was just turning to look at the house when the front door opened and a blonde wearing a white tennis outfit and holding a racket stepped out and came down the front steps. She saw me and motioned for me to come over. So I did.

As I approached I gave her a good look. She was tall but curvy, like a Jim Lee drawing of Wonder Woman. She had implausibly long legs that seemed even longer coming out from under her short skirt. They ended in ankle high socks and white and lavender Nikes. Though her legs were long she was not skinny, her arms looking nicely muscled but lean and her torso strong looking in her comfortable looking top. She was sort of busty as well and I reminded myself not to look at her breasts, although that top had a pretty deep neckline. At least try not to get caught, I told myself.

She had a Jim Lee body but more of a J. Scott Campbell *Danger Girl* face, all upturned little nose, smirky mouth and large, pretty blue eyes. She was very cute and very cute goes a long way with me.

I walked up to her and she offered a hand.

"Thank you Mr. Farrar for coming out, we appreciate it," she said, smiling. She had a good, strong handshake.

"Please. Call me William," I said. Suave.

We went up the steps and stood in the archway of the massive wooden front door. It looked like oak. It probably weighed more then my ride.

I threw a thumb back over my shoulder in the direction of my car-washing pal and said, "Friendly guy."

Jessica rolled her eyes and lowered her voice, though we were a good distance away. "Rick. Yeah, he's not a warm and fuzzy guy. My dad knew his dad and gave him a job." She lowered her voice even more and shook her head. "I'm not a fan."

I chuckled and then motioned to her outfit. "So… going bowling?"

She laughed and it wasn't a polite one like from the phone conversation but a good, heartfelt one. "Yes, I thought I'd sneak a few frames in. And then maybe - just MAYBE - I'd try a little tennis."

"That's crazy talk."

She laughed again and seemed to completely relax. She looked looser, more comfortable.

"Wow. You've been here, what? Thirty seconds? And you're a billion times more likable than the last guy dad called in. He was creepy as shit." Then she blushed and ducked her head. "Excuse my language." she said, clearly embarrassed.

I smiled and said, "Not a problem." Woman cursing never bothered me. My mother swore like a sailor. But it was the other thing she had said that was interesting.

"The last guy?" I asked. "Who was that?"

She seemed to tighten up a little again. "I better let my father tell you all that. Come on. He's in the sunroom."

Sunroom.

We walked through the big oak door and into the foyer which was a little smaller than my whole apartment and then down a cool, tile lined hall. A massive set of stairs to my right climbed upwards, probably to the rest of the museum. On the left, after the entrance to a giant living room or sitting room or whatever the hell they called it, we came to pictures in large frames adorning the walls. One caught my eye and I stopped. It was a photograph of two women smiling, both sitting across from each other in ornate chairs. They were holding hands and looking into the camera. They both seemed genuinely happy. They were identically dressed in rose colored blouses and dark skirts, their hair and jewelry exactly the same. Jessica looked just like, well, both of them. She gazed at the photograph for a second, a small smile on her face.

"My mother. And my aunt. This will stun you but... they

were twins."

I gave faux amazement. "No! More crazy talk."

She gave a smaller laugh this time and seemed to lose herself in the photo for a second. "My mother died in a car accident 6 years ago." She almost whispered. " And my aunt, well.... she just seemed to not care after that. It sounds corny but... she just lost the will to live, it seemed. She was gone 4 months later."

I'd lost both of my parents and I know what that empty feeling is like. When you lose your mother especially, you almost feel like the rope that connected you to everything was gone. "I'm sorry."

She smiled a little. "It's not your fault." Then a serious look crossed her face. "Wait. It's not your fault, is it?"

She had me for a second but I caught on. "No, I swear." I said, hands rose. "Not my fault. I promise!"

She laughed again and seemed better. "Oh, good. Cause then we would have a problem." She started down the hall again. I chuckled and followed. Funny girl.

We headed back farther into the house, through an amazing kitchen and back further still, until I could see the expansive back yard. It had to be at least 30 yards deep and almost that wide. About forty feet back from the house in the shade of an enormous tree was a beautiful wooden gazebo, big enough for maybe ten people to sit in comfortably. I could see myself out there on nice days, reading, having a drink, relaxing, with a nice breeze keeping me cool. Unfortunately a gazebo in my backyard was probably not in my near future. Actually, a backyard was probably not in my near future. I took another look at it and kept following.

We turned left and then right again and entered a glass and aluminum addition to the house. The sunroom. You could look up and see the sky where it showed between the canopy of leaves over it. There were tons of plants in the sunroom, tall exotic looking ones that reached almost to the angled ceiling, soaking up the filtered sunlight. In the right hand corner of the room there was a glass table that sat between two bamboo chairs with thick beige cushions. And in one of the chairs sat a man.

"Dad?" said Jessica as we approached. "This is William Farrar. William, this is my father, Coleman Chandler."

He seemed impossibly old to me, especially to have a daughter so young. Chandler sat with his spindly legs straight out, his hands on his lap. He was very thin. The sky blue sweater he wore seemed at least three sizes too big and the collar of the white shirt under came up and out like the wings on a big paper plane. The age spotted skin of his hands and face seemed stretched way too tight over his bones and skull. His nose was thin and sharp, jutting out almost defiantly at you. The mouth was a chisel cut in white plaster, just barely pink on the edges. He still had hair but it was bone white and combed back on his head. It was thicker than I would have thought, rising up and then back, not just lying on his skull like thread. But his eyes… even from where I was standing I could see that his eyes radiated life and energy. They were a clear blue like his daughter's but even more sharp and piercing. A lot was going on behind there. This dude still had his faculties. Almost as if to illustrate that, Chandler got up quickly from his seat and stuck out a hand.

"Mr. Farrar. A pleasure to meet you."

"Please," I said, shaking his hand. "Call me Will."

He gave me a good strong handshake and then sat again, motioning towards the other seat. I took him up on his offer. I was pleasantly surprised that he had no reaction to me being black. I've watched people embarrass themselves by trying too hard not to acknowledge it or by saying something that stupidly pointed it out. But Chandler seemed to not be surprised or have any issue with it. Maybe he knew already. I liked to think that he didn't.

"Would you like something, Will? A drink? A snack?" asked Jessica.

"No, I'm good, thank you." I settled deeper into the thick cushion. This chair was seriously comfortable. The room was a nice temperature, not too warm, not too cool. It was quiet except for our voices. If Mr. Chandler nodded off during our chat I probably wouldn't be too far behind him.

"Ok, well, then I'm off. "said Jessica. She took a little swing with the racket and struck a pose. "Strike!"

She and I laughed and then laughed even more at Mr. Chandler's confused look. After she walked out, Chandler looked at me and said, "I love her to pieces but sometimes I don't understand her at all."

I smiled at that and then we started talking about comic art.

2

"So. Mr. Farrar," said Coleman Chandler before taking a sip of whatever it was he was drinking. He swallowed and placed the glass back down on the table. "Tim Miller told me good things about you. I wish I had spoken to him earlier."

"Tim's a good guy," I said. Tim actually was a good guy. I've known him for years and I've sold him or found for him a lot of good art. I'd last spoke to him about a month ago concerning a Mike Mignola *Hellboy* page he was looking for. I managed to track it down and hook him up with the owner. Worked out well. When I thought about it, Tim owed me a few favors. Maybe this was payback for one of them.

Chandler nodded and leaned back in his wicker chair. He thoughtfully eyed me for a few seconds.

"What do you know about Curt Swan, Mr. Farrar?"

I leaned back in my seat too and thought about that for a minute, sorting it all out.

"Well, let's see," I said. "I know he started on *Superboy* in the late forties. Then he took over *Superman's Pal Jimmy Olsen* in the mid-fifties. His Superman pretty much became the DC "house" style, replacing Wayne Boring's version. I know that he worked on just about every Superman book DC had until about the mid-eighties when DC more or less fired him. Which wasn't cool. He drew that great Alan Moore story *"Whatever Happened To The Man Of Steel"* and some other stuff after that but he basically got pushed aside for newer artists. And then he died in.... '96, I think."

Chandler nodded appreciatively. "You know a good amount about him."

"Kinda my job to know that stuff."

He grunted slightly and shook his head. "You would be surprised at how few people know what they should know for their jobs."

I couldn't argue with that so I stayed quiet. Chandler took a sip from his glass and set it back down.

"Well, I will tell you a few things you don't know. Like, Curt Swan was a friend of mine. Well, he was a friend of mine and another man, who was my oldest friend. A man named Stewart Carvell. Stewart and I grew up in Princeton

Township. A lot of people thought we came from money. We really didn't… we were just fortunate enough to have fathers with businesses that had survived the Depression. By the time both of us had been born in 1943, those businesses were doing fairly well. And as the oldest boys, Stewart and I were like princes, heirs to the family business thrones. We didn't mind though. That was our fate and we didn't hate it. It was just the way it was."

Chandler stopped to take another sip of his drink and I used that time to do the quick math, which admittedly, wasn't that difficult. Born in 1943 meant that he was 71 years old. Jesus, I actually thought he was older than that by at least ten years. But 70 was nothing to sneeze at either.

Chandler set his glass back down and continued. "But Stewart and I shared, while growing up, a common love. Comic books. We just loved them. We read *Detective Comics* and *World's Finest* and the Timely books and the EC books… everything. We just were in awe of the artwork, in awe of these artists ability to bring these crazy stories to life. And our mothers taking those EC books away from us and throwing them out just made us want to read more of them. They weren't corrupting us like that idiot Wertham wrote. They were grand entertainment and escapism to two boys who had their lives already mapped out for them. Even through college - Princeton, of course - Stewart and I kept reading them, kept loving them. By then Timely had become Marvel and a whole new interest came about in these new super-heroes that lived in New York - in a real city - and had all these problems that you could actually relate to. And Kirby…" he paused and shook his head in awe. "Jack Kirby completely blew us away. The power, the dynamism of his art. Amazing. It just leapt out at you. It was like 3D in a 2D book." He stopped and peered at me suspiciously. "Do you like Kirby?"

"Love him. I have four Kirby pages. Two *Black Panther* pieces, a *New Gods* and an *Invaders* cover. No Silver Age art, unfortunately."

"Hard to come by." Chandler said, relaxed again. "I thought you were going to say you hated Kirby. I would've asked you to leave."

"I wouldn't blame you." I said and we both laughed. I had apparently passed a little test there.

"Well, by then," Chandler continued, "Stewart and I were making trips to New York and getting to know the city better. Both of our father's businesses were there so we prepping ourselves. Feeling out the town before we were expected to be there everyday. I believe it was 1962 or '63, when Stewart and I met Curt Swan at a cocktail party in Midtown. We were star struck. The artist of *Action Comics* and *Superman*, both of which we still read, was standing right in front of us and he was a great guy. Modest, nice, engaging… everything you would want your heroes to be. He seemed almost amused by the fanboy reaction he got from two Princeton students, both A students and on the honor roll. But he never spoke down to us and even befriended us. Sometime after that he invited us out to his house in Connecticut and showed us his studio. That's when we first saw the cover to *Action Comics* #305. Are you familiar with it?"

"Not off the top of my head, no."

Chandler frowned. "Yes, of course. I'm sorry. I hit you with a very vague reference there. I'll show it to you later. It's Clark Kent changing into Superman but he's being viewed through a two way mirror buy some gangsters. One has sold his secret identity to the others for a millions dollars. And one of the men has a box with a chunk of gold Kryptonite in it."

I shook my head. "I love those crazy old DC stories. They had, like, 10 different types of Kryptonite that had ten different effects on Superman."

"Yes," Said Chandler amused. "They did get a little carried away with all the Kryptonite." He thought for a second and then adjusted himself in his chair. "Anyway, we saw that cover in the unfinished pencils, sitting on Swan's drawing table. And it was beautiful. Stewart and I just fell in love with it. Then a few months later and I don't know how, Swan got his hands on the original, fully inked version. I don't know the story behind that. DC and Marvel never gave those pages back to the creators then but somehow he had it in his possession. He knew we loved the cover though and I don't remember how this came about but he offered to give the page to either Stewart or me. We couldn't decide who would get it so we played a game of Gin Rummy to decide. Winner got the cover. Forever."

He stopped and took another sip of his drink. He was playing it out, enjoying the drama. I could figure out who won the cover, though. At least, I thought. Maybe I was wrong. Now I wasn't so sure. He actually had me leaning forward in my chair, waiting on this little cliffhanger he had going.

Chandler put the drink down and leaned back slowly. Oh, boy. He was loving this. I tried to look like I didn't care but I'm sure hanging on the edge of my seat like that was a big giveaway.

"I lost." he said.

"Ah," I said after I had pulled myself back from the tip of my chair. He really got me with that story. "That must've been kind of upsetting."

Chandler smiled.

"You know, at first I was kind of upset. But then I quickly realized how silly I was being. My best friend, who I saw everyday, had won a great prize. I realized that not only should I be happy for him but, selfishly, I could see the page whenever I wanted. He was for all intents and purposes my brother. And so, for 40 years if I wanted to see it I could. It didn't matter who had won it."

Chandler stopped and his face darkened. It really was like that old saying "a cloud came over him". Any hint of humor and nostalgia disappeared from him and was replaced by a deep sadness. You could just see it. And right then, I knew what he was going to say next.

"Stewart Carvell died five weeks ago," said Chandler, trying very hard to stay toneless and unemotional. "Pancreatic Cancer. It was very quick."

I had an aunt who had died from Pancreatic Cancer. Brutal. You barely had time to celebrate this person's life while they were here before they were gone.

"I'm sorry. To lose a friend after so long...." I stopped, not knowing where I was going. Probably just making it worse. "I'm sorry." I repeated. What more could I say?

Chandler nodded slowly. He said "Thank you." and then just seemed to go elsewhere. He was still sitting in his chair but was clearly out of body, off in another time and place. I just let him stay wherever he was, feeling whatever he was feeling and checked out the sunroom some more. I couldn't imagine having a room like this, all glass enclosed and temperature controlled. The room faced west so you got the majority of sun at the end of the day. I could imagine reading by the setting sun, the room all vibrant gold and orange. I would be out here all the time. Between this and the gazebo, I would never see the rest of the house. Damn, it was good to have money. I sighed and looked out into the backyard. Somewhere out in the distance a dog barked. Probably upset that his Perrier bowl was empty.

Chandler stirred a bit, as if waking from a nod off. He refocused on me and cleared his throat.

"Tethers, Mr. Farrar. Those lifelines that keep you living. I've lost another. My parents, my wife, Stewart… after a while you just want to cut the remaining ropes and float away too. Go be with those that you miss. You understand?"

"I do. But I'm sure Jessica wouldn't like that kind of talk."

Chandler smiled. "Yes. You're right, I do have my daughters as tethers. Though one is much tighter than the other. Still lifelines, I suppose. So, somewhat reluctantly, I will keep living. And you can help me reclaim something that will help with that."

Getting to the nitty gritty. I didn't know what this would entail but already it was sounding a little more convoluted than I was used to.

"Stewart left the Swan cover to me in his will." said Chandler. He stopped and took another sip of his drink. Man, this guy could make a glass of something last.

"It was the only thing he left me. We both had done very well so I didn't need or want anything else. He kept the cover in a sealed black frame, very well taken care of and preserved. After the will was read Stewart's wife, Erin – wonderful woman – and I agreed on a day to pick it up. So a week ago, I sent a gentleman who works for me, Rick… did you meet Rick?"

I smiled. "Yes. I met him."

"Alright. Good man. Problems in the past but I saw something in him. Anyway, I sent Rick down to Cherry Hill, where Stewart lived, to get the cover. It's a long trip and it's very difficult for me to be in a car for that long. Just too uncomfortable. Going down for Stewart's funeral was almost unbearable. So Rick drove down, retrieved the cover and began back. But he pulled into a rest stop in Freehold to get some food and go to the bathroom. And the Bentley was broken into."

"Wow. Was this at night?" I asked.

"No. Broad daylight. Probably about two in the afternoon."

"Ballsy."

"Very."

"And they took the cover."

Chandler nodded, his mouth a tight line. "Yes, along with a camera that Rick had in the car. And his phone."

"That's a hell of a coincidence," I said. "You just get the cover and a little while later someone breaks into your car in broad daylight and steals it?"

"Well, he was driving the Bentley. I probably should've asked him to drive a more discreet vehicle. Probably somebody hanging out at the rest stop, waiting for nice cars to roll in."

"I guess. And you think someone maybe sold the cover and now it's back on the market."

"I'm hoping. It has value and would probably fetch a decent amount but it's of greater sentimental value to me. I called Erin after it was stolen and she was as upset as I was. It meant so much to Steve and to me. If it's out there I want it. I will go above the market price to retrieve it. Well above."

I thought about who I could reach out to. There were a lot of people who might've gotten their hands on it or who heard about it. I didn't want to float the whole "go above market price" thing for it to anybody at first. That was just asking to get gouged.

"Ok." I said. "I can ask around. Probably not a lot of Curt Swan covers floating around for sale."

"Well, it's a remarkable cover piece," said Chandler. "It should get a lot of attention."

I nodded my head slowly.

"I guess."

"Why, Mr. Farrar," said Chandler, smiling. "Are you not a Curt Swan fan?"

"He's a good artist. Very good. I just tend to be more of a Win Mortimer guy myself."

Chandler's eyes bulged almost comically and he wagged a crooked finger at me. "Ah!" he said, "Ah! I knew I liked you, Mr. Farrar!"

He rose from his chair and headed towards the door leading back into the house. "Finally someone who will appreciate this! Come! Come!"

He led me out of the sunroom and just beyond the kitchen I saw a flash of movement. No details, just a human sized blur disappearing into the hall. Had Jessica not left yet? Was there someone else in the house?

We made our way to the staircase near the front door and then started up. Chandler was making good time as he but I could tell it was a chore. I listened as best I could but I didn't hear any movement besides ours.

"So," I said casually. "Is it just you and Jessica that lives here? Or does your other daughter live here too?"

"Jennifer? God, no. To be honest I have no idea where Jennifer lives. The last I heard she was out in California."

We stopped at the first landing and Chandler caught his breath. It was a pretty tall staircase.

"No," he said. "It's probably best that Jennifer doesn't live here anymore."

Yikes. Chandler turned, walked to the next set of steps (how big was this house???) and started up.

"Oh, and Rick." he said, stopping on the stairs to look at me. "Rick lives here, too."

"Ah."

Our pace had slowed but we finally made it to the next floor. Most of the doors leading to the rooms were closed but one at the east end of the house was open, daylight streaming out into the hall. After Chandler caught his breath we headed towards it.

We stepped through the door and I stopped when I saw everything. I just stopped and stared.

The room was a gallery. The floor was beautiful blond wood and bone colored walls held black framed artwork that took up all the wall space that the two big windows didn't. I turned to look and all I saw was comic art. From where I stood I could identify a Gil Kane *Green Lantern* cover, a Wally Wood EC science fiction page, a Will Eisner *Spirit* splash, a John Buscema *Conan* page…. he had artwork by some of my all time favorite comic artists, pieces that I could not afford to even hold much less own.

There were two rows of frames around the whole room, except for the wall at the north end, which had four rows. A small chair sat near that wall, so you could sit and see the art comfortably without bending. In the center of the room sat a tall flat file that served as a sort of desk, probably filled with art that hadn't been framed yet or art that wasn't quite wall worthy. On the flat file sat an empty frame, a John Romita *Spider-Man* page and a small slip of white paper.

Suddenly Chandler, who had been standing next to me and watching my reaction, hurried over to the flat file. He slid the Romita over with his left and placed his right over the slip of paper. If I hadn't noticed the paper in the first place I probably wouldn't have thought much about it.

"So, Mr. Farrar. What do you think?' he said, smiling.

"This is amazing. This art… just amazing. Can I look around?"

"Of course! Feel free!"

I slipped to my right, half looking at a Berni Wrightson *Swamp Thing* splash and half watching Chandler out of the corner of my eye. He took the white slip of paper that he had palmed, folded it and opened a smaller top draw in the flat file. A quick glance at me, where I played up my analyzing of the *Swamp Thing* art, and then he dropped the paper into the drawer and quietly closed it.

Hmmm.

I decided to let that slide for a bit and just appreciate the art. Next to the Swamp Thing was a Batman page from the short but legendary Steve Englehart/Marshall Rogers run on *Detective Comics,* featuring the Joker in the story *"The Laughing Fish"*. And next to that was the cover to *Batman* #84, which was done by Win Mortimer. In fact, the three covers next to that one were all Win Mortimer pieces. There was *Detective Comics* #267, which was the first appearance of Bat-Mite, the classic *Superman* #76, which featured Superman and Batman both swooping in to save Lois Lane from atop a burning building and *Superman* #74, which depicted Lex Luthor turning Supes and Lois into stone with some kind of machine.

I had never seen the original art to these, only the scanned color art online or reproduced in a DC collection. Seeing it in black and white like this, with all its tiny revisions and whited out spots and pasted on masthead was like a revelation to me. You always appreciate comic art more when you see the originals and this made me like

Mortimer even more. At DC in the 40's and 50's they had a lot of artists like Swan and Al Plastino and Wayne Boring but I always liked Mortimer better. His covers were always more kinetic to me, with interesting angles and a slight canting of the characters to add some movement. I was just blown away looking at them.

"I thought you might like these." said Chandler, smiling.

"I'm just amazed. I can't believe you have this art." I turned around and scanned the whole gallery. There were two Curt Swan *Superman* covers next to the Mortimer pieces and a great Jack Cole *Plastic Man* page next to those. There were more great pieces that I hadn't even gotten to yet, a lot more. "I can't believe this whole damn room."

Chandler laughed and at the same time I heard a floorboard or step creak out in the hall. I looked out but saw, as I expected, nothing. Then I heard another slight creak, lower this time. Somebody walking down the stairs, trying to be silent. Boy, there seemed to be some curious stuff going on in this house. Which reminded me of something.

"Oh sorry," I said, reaching into my pocket. "Just got a text. Was expecting one from my landlord." I took my phone out and pretended to read. "Yeah, it's from him. Sorry." I said again.

"That's alright," said Chandler.

"No, I didn't want to seem rude. Just something important I had to look at."

I backed up to the flat file, very clearly put my iPhone down and then turned slightly so that Chandler couldn't see me sliding it under the Romita page.

"You - and this great, great room - have my undivided attention now." I said.

Chandler laughed again. "No, I understand. It's no problem. Things crop up. But I appreciate you doing that. Look around some more and then we'll discuss the Swan cover further. I just thought you would appreciate this."

"I definitely do. Thank you!"

I started going around the room, counter clockwise, circling towards the two windows that faced the front of the house. I looked out and down and saw Rick walking back towards the Bentley, coming from the direction of the front door. He looked up at the gallery windows, saw me and then tried to play it off as if he just happened to be staring up in the sky, like he was checking out the weather or trying to find Jupiter. I stopped myself from laughing and turned my attention back to the art. The two pieces after the first window were from *Avengers Annual* #10, the classic comic that introduced the future X-Man Rogue and may be, arguably, one of the single greatest illustrated issues of a comic ever. A complete home run by artist Michael Golden, one of my favorites, every page and every panel is outstanding. Next to those were a Golden *Batman Family* page and a Golden *Micronauts* page, two more jaw droppers. And then, right next to them, was Jack Kirby.

The first two were Captain America pages inked by Joe Sinnott, one showing Cap just wearing out some goons in typical kinetic Kirby fashion. The second featured the Black Panther, who Kirby and Lee had introduced in the *Fantastic Four* in 1965 and then paired him with Cap in 1968 in the *Tales of Suspense* comic right before it became Captain America's own book. The two of them were beating up some of Baron Zemo's goons out in the jungle. Kirby just went to town on fight scenes. You could really feel these poor punks getting their heads put out looking at those panels. There was another Kirby Cap page next to those, a great fight scene between Cap and a robot Steve Rogers, Cap's alter ego. That one was inked by Frank Giacoa. But below that and to the left, the wall was empty, a space for three frames of art.

"I'm actually jealous that you have Silver Age Kirby art," I said. "But what happened here? Changing the frames on some?"

Chandler smiled slightly. "No, just arranging to get more art for that space."

"Kirby?"

"Yes."

"Nice."

I was going to continue the tour – I could see a Rafael Grampa Batman piece across the room that was killing me – but I changed my mind.

"You know, I am truly loving this room but I would be in here all day. Let's talk about that Swan cover and how I can help you with that."

"Are you sure? There's plenty of art left for you to look at."

"Is there a time limit on looking at this art that I don't know about?", I smiled, making it clear that I was joking. "When I bring your cover back do I have to put it through the mail slot? What's up?"

Chandler laughed. "No, no time limit. You're right. Let's discuss the cover. I am anxious to get it back."

"So I take it that you brought in somebody with some background in this to search for the page."

All humor drained from Chandler's face. "Yes. After getting some particularly bad advice from an auctioneer I know, I approached an overweight, unpleasant gentleman by the name of Donnie Castiglia to look for it. Do you know him?"

"Yes, I know him," I said, trying hard not to smile. Anyone who knew Donnie would say that calling him an overweight, unpleasant gentleman was a compliment. Donnie was basically a straight up asshole to most people. To me, he was just a pain in the ass. Probably because I limited my interaction with him as much as I could. But he had a working relationship with one of the guys at Legacy Auctions, the biggest high-end comic art dealer.

"Was that auctioneer a guy named Jerry Ryback?" I asked.

Chandler just nodded.

"Yeah, Donnie's been directing sellers to him forever. Both of them can be tough to deal with," I said. "What happened?"

"Mr. Castiglia tried to take advantage of my feelings for that cover. He told me that he knew of its whereabouts but he would need a large amount of money to secure it. He also said that it was a "delicate situation" that required "additional funds" to pay off some information. I didn't believe him and told him he was done. But realistically I can't stop him from locating the art and dangling it over my head. So I really need you to find it first, Mr. Farrar."

I thought about all the connections I had and the information I had access to. I could probably put the feelers out and get a response in a decent amount of time. But Donnie had those same connections and a head start on me. I could only assume, since he hadn't held the art hostage yet, that he didn't have the cover. So unfortunately, it hadn't been that easy to track down. Luckily, some people I know plain old refused to deal with Donnie so that was an advantage I had. But word would probably get back to him that I was snooping around for the same page. Something told me that, although I would be tipping my hand, I would have to take the direct approach with Donnie. Ugh.

"I'll dig around, see if there's anything he missed." I said. "Knowing him, he got sloppy on a few things. I'll find it."

"Good man." said Chandler. He reached into his back pocket, pulled out a wallet and produced a thick wad of bills from it. I could see 100's on them. He counted off ten and placed them on the flat file.

"That's a… retainer, I guess you could say. You will get two thousand more when you find the page. Get the price down to as reasonable a cost as you can. A very reasonable price will get a bonus that you and I will negotiate at that time but I will tell you that it will be another thousand dollars or more. And I thought you might appreciate getting cash instead of a check. Acceptable?"

I picked up the hundreds, folded them and put them in my pocket. This man just gave me a grand and told me I had two more waiting for me. And extra money for getting a good price for it. Acceptable?

"Very. I'll get that page for you, Mr. Chandler."

"Excellent." Chandler smiled, stuck his hand and I shook it. "If you need anything, call my daughter and she will help you as best as she can."

"Alright."

He led me through the door of the gallery and back towards the staircase. I waited until we were almost to the stairs, and then made a show of patting my jean pockets.

"Damn, I left my phone in your gallery." I said, trying to look apologetic. "I'll just be a second."

I didn't wait for a response and hurried back into the gallery, making sure Chandler couldn't see me from his angle. I went around the large center table and quietly opened the drawer that he had dropped the folded paper in. Yeah, that was pretty damn nosy of me but he had really piqued my interest with that move. I had to know what it said. I took the paper out, unfolded it and read.

Handwritten on the paper were the numbers 48, 49 and 50.

That was disappointing. I don't know what I expected, like it was going to say, "All my money is hidden in my mattress" or "I know where Jimmy Hoffa is buried." Something interesting, at least. I didn't know what the hell 48, 49 and 50 had to do with anything.

I refolded the slip of paper and put it back in the drawer, silently closing it while I picked up my phone. Chandler was just reaching the door as I was.

"Got it. I'm always misplacing this thing."

"No problem."

He didn't seem suspicious at all. We headed back to the stairs and suddenly Chandler seemed tired. Worn out. He stopped, leaned heavily against the thick wooden bannister and said, "That's right, Jessica left."

"Its alright, Mr. Chandler, I can find me way out." I said. It was pretty much straight down to the front door, no twists or turns. I just hoped that Chandler didn't think I would go apeshit in the house once I was out of his sight.

On the contrary, he seemed relieved. "Thank you." he said wearily. He took a breath and pushed himself up. "Think I'll rest a bit." Wow. Chandler had appeared to be resting when I first met him. He must have used up a lot of energy and adrenalin just going over the details and talking about comic art. I watched him head slowly towards what must have been a bedroom and frowned. Getting old is a bitch.

I walked down the two flights of stairs, past the photograph of Mrs. Chandler and her sister, through the giant foyer and out the front door. The black Audi was gone and Rick was kneeling by the grill of the Bentley and waxing, trying to look busy. He had positioned himself so that he could see me as he "worked". I waved and said, "Car looks great, Rick!"

Rick stood slowly, tossed the rag on the hood of the Bentley and just stared. So. No death-match it seemed but something else was totally confirmed: yet another Christmas card I wouldn't be getting.

I got in the Jeep and drove off, a still scowling Rick receding in my rear view mirror.

3

I drove a little ways and then made a left on South Orange Avenue and a right onto Sloan Street, which is where the New Jersey Transit South Orange train station is. There was a parking spot right in front of where I wanted to go but discovered that the comic book store I remembered was long gone and was now a restaurant named Stony's. I looked it up online and it seemed to have well regarded burgers so I took my being here as a sign and went in. The place was decorated with model airplanes and old pictures of fighter jets and bombers. Even the burgers were getting in on the act with "Fighters" being single patty and "Bombers" being double. I ordered a bomber with American cheese, mushrooms and raw onions and a Pepsi and looked at the pictures and read the captions as I waited. Somebody was a real fighter pilot buff in here. Soon they called my number and I took a seat by the large window facing the street and looked out at the elevated train platform across the way. South Orange station had a nice, small town feel to it. It was all sand-colored stone and forest green painted metal bannisters, all very old-school and classic. A New Jersey transit train rumbled to a stop, waited for a few moments and then churned away. People were going in and out of the Coldstone Creamery and Starbucks that was beneath the station. A bakery next to Starbucks was doing good business as well. Some kids, who looked like they should've been in school, were skateboarding in the little plaza that fronted it all. I ate my food slowly and watched it all happen. It had gotten warmer and whoever could be out was out and enjoying it.

While I ate I thought about Coleman Chandler. That gallery he had of comic art was absolutely amazing. I would love to have some of those pieces. And he knew his comics, too. He seemed really passionate about that Swan cover and I wanted to find it for him. The three grand plus he was offering didn't hurt either. It was nice to have motivation in multiple forms.

I finished by cheeseburger and fries and was drinking

my Pepsi when it occurred to me that I was delaying something that I really didn't want to do. I knew I had to speak to Donnie Castiglia but I'd actually rather go to the DMV. First thing on a Monday morning. But to get a full picture of this story I had to talk to him, which pissed me off. I sat there and fumed for a few seconds and then went through the contacts on my iPhone. There was the number. I took a deep breath, tried to think of another way and dialed. Maybe he wouldn't answer. Maybe it would go to voicemail and then when he called me back I would let that go to voicemail and that way I could find out what I needed without ever having to speak with him. And maybe Superman would fly through the wall, give me the art, say, "I heard you were looking for this." and fly away. That was probably more likely.

After the second ring, there was a scratching, rustling noise from the other end and then a pause. Damn. Then a voice.

"Farrar, you fuck. What do you want? You know what, never mind what you want. You never come out to the store. So fuck you."

I sighed. "I'm good, Donnie, thanks. How are you?"

"Screw that. I'm in Williamsburg. You live, like, fifteen minutes from here. It's not like I'm way the fuck up in the Bronx. Asshole."

I lived a lot more than 15 minutes away but I really didn't feel like arguing the point. I didn't feel like speaking to him at all but here we were.

"I never get up that way, Donnie. But I'll come up there soon. Seriously."

That seemed to appease him momentarily. "Whatever. What do you want?"

"I understand you were looking for a Superman page for Coleman Chandler. Sorry it didn't go well but he wants me to pick up the ball now."

"Oh, so I'm officially fired now, huh? Chandler hired the Black Private Dick to track it down." Donnie grunted. "Well, fine. Let you deal with it. I bet you'll nail that hot piece of ass daughter of his, too. I can't stand you, man."

I sighed again and rubbed my face. Talking with Donnie was always like this. It was always 95% insults and bullshit and 5% useful information. I really just wanted to bail on the whole conversation but had no choice but to keep fighting through it.

"Ok, so how far did you get with this?"

"Oh, right. I'm just supposed to up and tell you what I know. You get the big check and I'm left holding my dick. Fuck you. I know you probably have a lead already. Get the last bit of info out of me and kick me to the curb with nothing. You lying, thieving, backstabbing fuck."

"Wow."

His laugh was humorless. "Yeah. Went there."

I was starting to get really, really annoyed but I pushed that back down and stayed calm. "Dude, I just walked into this movie. I don't have any info to tell you much less hold back from you. If what you tell me is helpful then I'll cut you in. Seriously."

"Bullshit. Would you believe me if I told you that?"

"No. Because you're a fucking scumbag. I'm the honest one here."

It was quiet for a second. "Damn."

"Yeah. Went there."

It was quiet again. I thought I might've pushed it too far but fuck it. He was getting on my nerves. Then Donnie laughed.

"Fuckin' Farrar. You're funny."

He laughed some more and then coughed. "Ok, what do you want to know?"

I shook my head. This guy was out there. "Well, I just need to know how far you tracked this."

"It was kinda easy, actually, up to a point," said Donnie. "I asked around and somebody told me that Poon had just bought a Superman cover and it sounded like the one I was describing. So I called him up and, sure enough, that was the one."

Poon was Ken Tang, a really cool dude from Queens who was in the same comic art business as the rest of us. Ken was smart, a good guy and seriously unfortunate to have the last name Tang around a bunch of immature knuckleheads like us. Hence the nickname, "Poon". He had a good sense of humor so he was pretty good about it. But everybody called him Poon to the point that it seemed natural. I barely remembered not to call him it.

"Oh, so Poon has it," I said. See? Really difficult to not say it. "So what's the problem?"

"Well, he sold it. That's what he said anyway. He told me that a guy named Michael Rothstein from Jersey bought it from him. But when I told him that I needed to get touch with the guy he couldn't remember his contact info or how he hooked up with him." Donnie sounded a tad disbelieving when he said that. "Didn't sound right to me. So I say fine and hang up. As it turns out I know a guy out there who knows Michael so I got his number and called him up. This guy Michael is a big Superman nut. Buys all kinds of Big Blue shit. And he says that Poon sold him a couple pages, yeah, but only one was a Swan piece and neither one was a cover."

"Huh." I said.

"Yeah, that's how I was. So I call Poon back up and I'm like, Yo, Poon, you sent me on a wild goose chase, what the fuck? And he was all like, Oh, I think I sold it to this other guy who was from California or maybe some other dude, I don't remember. Which I call bullshit on 'cause Poon remembers everything."

I had to give Donnie that one because Poon really did have a great memory for things. And not just what issue did Phoenix first appear in the *X-Men* or how long was Mark Waid's run on the *Flash*, either. He remembered everything it seemed like. One time we were just chatting outside of Jim Hanley's Universe and I started telling this story about driving through Virginia during a snowstorm and Poon recalled that my mother was from Charlottesville, which I didn't even remember ever telling him. So it did seem a little odd that he suddenly couldn't remember who he sold a page to.

"Yeah, that is kinda weird." I said. "So you think this Rothstein guy is being legit?"

"Yeah, definitely. He told me everything I wanted to know, he was real upfront about it. Poon was the one acting nervous and shit. Besides, why would he lie about it?"

"So you think Poon was lying?"

Donnie sighed. "I don't know. I don't get why he would. But he was acting really strange. The whole thing was just weird."

I didn't have anything to add to that so I said, "Ok. Well,

do me a favor and text me that Rothstein guys number."

It was quiet on Donnie's end for a second and then he said, "What, you don't believe me? You think I'm making shit up, Farrar?"

"Jesus Christ, man, take it easy," I said, exasperated. "I'm just following up. Maybe this guy can remember something that'll help find it. Don't be so fucking defensive."

"Ok, ok," Donnie muttered, in what would be his closest attempt at an apology. "I'll send it to you later. When I get to it."

"Fine," I said, rolling my eyes. Always has to seem like he's in control. I wasn't originally going to ask my next question but Donnie was being such a fucking jerk that I had to hear his version of it. "So what happened with you and Chandler?"

Donnie sucked his teeth. "Man, fuck that old, cheap bastard. He was going on and on about that fucking page. It means so much to me and it's a reminder of better times, blah, blah, blah. But he only wants to pay two grand to find it?"

I held back the urge to tell him that I was getting three grand and said, "Well, shit, Donnie, that's just two grand to find the page. That wasn't even a cut of the final sale, yet. You were guaranteed that."

"Did you go to his house? That fuckin' guy is loaded,

dude. He could definitely come across with more than that. So I said fuck it, he's gonna have to. Is that wrong?"

"Uh… yeah."

"OH, I forgot. I'm talking to Johnny Morals here, Mr. Do The Right Thing. Well, I got a store to run, Farrar. I need all the cash I can get. So I held out for more. Fuck Chandler, man and fuck you. I gotta eat too."

I guess Donnie thought I just lived on oxygen and water or some shit, like he was the only one who needed to eat. I just let that one go though, because I was honestly getting tired. I tried to think of anything else to get out of him because I really didn't want to call back. "So that was all Poon said? Nothing else helpful?"

"No, that was it. He was real mysterious," Donnie paused a second, like something was coming to him. "Oh! But get this. Poon said a hot chick sold it to him. A hot BLONDE chick."

I waited but Donnie didn't say anything else.

"Ok. I'm not sure I'm following you." I said.

"A hot blonde chick and her father are looking for this cover. And it just so happens that ANOTHER hot blonde chick sold the very same cover? Come on."

"So… you're saying that Jessica Chandler sold the very same page to Poon that her father is looking to buy? That doesn't make any sense, Donnie."

"I don't know!" he said, annoyed. "Maybe she found the page first but needed the money and sold it. And she never told her dad. And now he'll buy it and she'll still have her money. See?"

"She would've had to have bought the page in the first place. Why spend the money if she didn't have to? And why would she sell it at all? If she had it she could've just told her dad she knew where it was, take his money like she was making the deal and just give him the page." I put my head down on the table. This guy can be fucking impossible to reason with sometimes.

"Why am I even thinking about this?" I said. "It's just a coincidence, that's all. There's more than just one cute blonde in the world, dude."

"I don't know, man.... There's just some weird shit with this art. There's a lot more to this cover than we know."

I picked my head up at that comment. "What the hell does that mean?" I asked.

There was a long pause on the other end. I could hear sounds in the background through the phone so I just waited.

Finally Donnie spoke. "A guy came to my store the other day."

"Ok."

Another pause. Then: "He.... strongly suggested that if I

found the cover that I should contact him first."

I frowned at my phone. Across the street one of the kids took a nasty spill on his skateboard and his friends laughed at him. He struggled to his feet and gave them the finger. I stifled a laugh, remembered that Donnie was telling me some nonsense and said, "A guy."

"Yeah, some guy. I never seen him before. I was by myself and he was kinda threatening me and then two guys that work for me came back from lunch and he left."

"So you're telling me that some guy came into your store and tried to shake you down for a Superman cover," I tried not to sound sarcastic but I didn't try hard. "That's what you're telling me."

"Fuck you, Farrar, that's what happened," He sucked his teeth. "Man...."

I sighed. "Ok, What did he look like?" Maybe it was short muscle guy. That would be interesting.

"Uh.... tall, maybe 6′ 2″. Big. Long hair. Big jaw."

Nope, not short muscle guy. Fucking Donnie. He almost had me.

"Come on, man."

"That's what fuckin' happened, man!" Donnie snapped angrily. "When he looks you up, don't say I didn't tell you. Asshole."

"Ok, ok. I'll keep an eye out for him. How does this guy

know about the page in the first place?"

I could practically hear Donnie shrug. "Fuck I know? He just showed up at the store. I didn't take the time to fuckin' interview him. But I'm telling you, something is up with this shit, man. So, good luck."

Donnie paused for a moment, I guess for dramatic effect. "And watch your ass." he said and hung up.

4

I put my phone down on the counter and stared at it for a few minutes, trying to decide if Donnie was the biggest asshole I knew. Weight-wise I think he was, although there was this really fat guy I used to work with that was seriously annoying. But he was more bitchy and whiny than anything else, not so much an asshole. So weight wise, Donnie won. Non weight wise, just based on sheer assholishness, I knew of a few people that could probably give him a run for his money. Clearly, this required deeper consideration so I decided to put it off until later and called Poon, who I am proud to say is "Ken Tang" in my phone contacts and not "Poon". But neither answered and I left a message asking for him to give me a buzz back whenever. I then called a couple of people I knew who bought and dealt comic art. They knew nothing about a Curt Swan Superman cover but were suddenly interested. The dangers of spreading the word.

There were more leads I could've followed then but I decided to push them until tomorrow. After I finished my soda I checked my iPhone for the closest comic book store. If it were reasonably close by I would drive over. After dealing with knuckleheads like Donnie, the geek solace of thumbing through comics was sorely needed. It was Thursday and all the new books had come out the day before so my batch was already at home, half read. But there's always something to pick up from a comic store.

The nearest was a place called New World Manga in Livingston, which is the next town west of South Orange. It was maybe fifteen minutes from where I was. Sold. I got rid of my trash and stepped outside, taking in some sun. The skateboard kids were gone from across the street and there was no blood on the concrete so I guess they all survived. I guess.

On the way over I thought more about what Donnie had told me. Donnie was an All-World bullshitter, so I was not inclined to believe his little story about a leg-breaker trying to muscle in on a comic cover deal. It just sounded like nonsense to me. Was he trying to scare me off of this? To what end? I gave up trying to understand it; I'd end up in the nuthouse trying to get behind Donnie's reasoning. If some clown called me up and actually tried to brace me for a Curt Swan Superman cover then I guess that would show me.

New World Manga was in a little sort of strip mall on Mount Pleasant Ave, sharing the space with a diner, some other places that I did not immediately recognize just what their business was and a carwash. The car wash and the diner had some customers but overall it was pretty slow and quiet. It was even more so in New World Manga, which was fine by me. I definitely was not in the mood for a crowd of people. A guy named Lionel was running the place and we struck up a good conversation about DC's New 52 thing and Marvel NOW. Then we talked some classic comics, had a friendly disagreement over some artists and even threw some New York Jets in there. I bought two back issues of *Secret Avengers* that I completely missed and a new issue of *Conan,* which looked pretty damn nice. Good times. I actually felt bad when I had to tell Lionel that I always get my comics at Midtown in the city. Dude had presented a good case to be a regular customer but driving out to Livingston every week was not viable. I'd kill myself if I had to make that drive on the regular. I promised I would drop in now and then and left.

By the time I turned onto my block in Brooklyn it was well past four o'clock. There were a decent amount of parking spaces available as a lot of drivers weren't home yet and I found a spot a little down the street right behind a beautiful silver Audi R8. Wow, two R8's in the same day. I parked, got out and took a look at it. The R8 was a sleek little race car looking two-seater that probably would do zero to sixty in exactly how long it would take a person to say zero to sixty. And this was the V10, too. Ridiculous. This car had to be over $150,000. Definitely a visitor. I took one last look at it, apologized to my Jeep for staring and walked back to my place.

My building has a doorman named Pierre and he was standing out front as I approached. Pierre flashed me a wide smile when he saw me, one that was much wider than normal, and he closed the gap to meet me. Oh, boy. Somebody in my building must've done something interesting. Or stupid. Or both.

"You have company." he said. Pierre was Haitian and had a deep voice so even if he had said, "You have a can of peas." it still would've sounded cool.

"Oh, do I?"

"Yes. Very attractive company." he said, smiling even broader.

Huh. As we approached the front door I was trying to imagine who it was. There was one person I knew it couldn't be. Pierre would've said so. And I doubted that she would come back… though I had to admit that I wished she did.

Jessica Chandler was sitting on the visitors couch opposite Pierre's station, looking at her phone. She was wearing black jeans with a white button up blouse and a light black jacket over it, very simple but nice. She had on black open toe shoes with a little heel, not too much, and I could see her magenta painted toes. Her hair was a little different but I couldn't really place how. Maybe after tennis and everything she changed it a little. For some reason it looked different to me. After a second she realized that someone was watching her and she looked up. A smile lit up her face and she rose, extending a hand.

"Mr. Farrar, it's good to see you again."

"Will, please." I said, shaking her hand and smiling back. "What are you doing here? Not that I'm complaining."

She laughed a little and I glanced at Pierre, who was leaning against his little desk and clearly enjoying the whole thing. I frowned at him and he pretended to check his visitor's log.

"Well, I thought we could talk a little more about the cover and arrange a sort of check in schedule." Said Jessica, tucking her phone into a tiny bag that I didn't see before. "We didn't get a chance to talk."

"You could've called me, you didn't have to drive all the way out here. What if I didn't come back until late?"

She smiled at Pierre. "Well, I would've given my number to Pierre, who was a very nice host in your absence." I glanced at Pierre again and he seemed almost embarrassed, which was funny to me. "I didn't have your number on me. I called you from my father's phone the other night. So I wanted to give you my contact information… besides, I've never driven to Brooklyn before. I'd thought I'd be adventurous."

I laughed. "Adventurous would be leaving that Audi, which I assume is yours, out too late. You'd have another adventure walking home. What do you have, a collection of Audi's?"

Jessica slid up to me and put her hand lightly on my chest. I say slid because she didn't really seem to walk so much as she glided up to me. Her big blue eyes were right on target with mine. She had on a pretty smelling perfume I didn't recognize, but it was light and subtle.

"A few," she said coyly. "And you wouldn't let me walk home, would you?" Her voice was all was sweet and cute and sexy at the same time. I glanced at Pierre and almost burst out laughing when I saw his slack-jawed, big-eyed reaction.

"No, I wouldn't do that, you're right. I'm sure you could talk me into giving you a ride."

"In your car or…?" she teased.

"Wow."

"I'm sorry!" she said, laughing. "I am really out of control here. It's this Brooklyn air." She fanned herself and laughed again. "Forgive me."

"No problem at all. But we should probably talk about that "ride" upstairs. I think we're embarrassing Pierre."

She laughed again and as I steered her towards the elevator I snuck another glance at Pierre who was just staring at us, open-mouthed. I thought about how many questions I would have to answer or avoid later.

We passed the mailboxes and I thought briefly about checking mine but changed my mind. Mail suddenly didn't seem to be a priority at that moment. But I wasn't exactly sure if I were reading these vibes correctly and even if I was, I wasn't sure if it would be best to keep this as professional as possible. I didn't really see how anything that happened could complicate things but you never know. Sometimes it's better to not find out. I was weighing all that when the elevator opened before we got to it and Karen Carter, who lives down the hall from me, stepped out.

Karen is a hot mother of two who I guess you would classify as a cougar. She was over fifty but you wouldn't know it by looking at her; if I didn't know her I would've guessed maybe early forties. You could tell she had kids but she was a damn good looking woman, especially with the

Chestnut colored hair she had been rocking lately and the recent weight loss. Karen, come hell or high water, always, always, always hits on me. She is unrelenting, even knocking on my door with a loosely tied robe on and not a whole lot underneath. I'm not above getting with an older woman but her husband is a corrections officer and I did not need that kind of trouble. Her being married was bad enough. I know for a fact that all CO's are insane. I didn't need a crazy, enraged man with a gun knocking on my door at two in the morning. I would bet that most people didn't.

Karen smiled when she saw me but then she saw my hand on Jessica's elbow and the smile left her face. Oh, boy.

"Hi, Mrs. Carter." I said. I wasn't sure how this would go but I tried to start it off as cordial as possible. I didn't owe Karen anything but I knew that strolling into my apartment with a white girl raised the bar for potential nonsense.

"Well, aren't we formal," she said in a monotone voice, eyeing Jessica up and down. Nice. We were off to a good, chilly start. "Who's your friend?"

"Hi, I'm Jessica Chandler." said Jessica, all bright-eyed and bushy-tailed. Jesus. I didn't want introductions, I wanted hi's and goodbyes and out. Jessica stuck her hand out and said "And you are?"

There was a moment of absolute stillness, Jessica smiling, waiting for the shake and Karen looking at her hand like it was electrified. It seemed to last forever.

"Annoyed." said Karen and walked away.

Jessica looked at me and I rolled my eyes as I stopped the elevator doors from closing and hustled us in. I punched four and gave Jessica a headshake as I leaned against the back wall. Just before the doors closed I could see Pierre staring at me with a huge smile on his face.

"Hmmm." said Jessica. "I don't think your old lady girlfriend likes me."

"Stop."

"I bet this building is crawling with Farrar cougars. One for each floor?"

I laughed. "Two, actually. Except for the 8th, I've got three up there."

"Oh my God, not Mrs. Smithers, too? She's seventy five years old."

That one got me and I burst out laughing.

"Smartass. I got no girls in this building."

"Uh huh. Well, you need to tell your friend from the lobby that. She seems a tad possessive."

"A tad."

"So, William Farrar must have a lady friend somewhere, I imagine."

"Not at present."

"Oh. So William Farrar must've had a lady friend

recently?"

I opened my mouth to answer, thought about it and then closed it.

"Ah," she said. "A story."

"A story."

"Am I going to hear this story?"

The elevator got to four and the door opened.

"Not if I can help it." I said and escorted her out.

I guided her left and past two doors before we reached my apartment. I got my keys out and was about to open the door when I paused and looked at Jessica.

"I just wanted to warn you," I said, with mock seriousness. "There are wonders past this door. Amazing, fantastic things await you. You will be thrilled."

Jessica smirked and put a hand on her hip. "My, we're confident."

"Not me, silly. The apartment. My stuff."

"Oh. I messed that up, then. Ok, let me try again. Oh! Fantastic things, you say…?"

"Never mind, you ruined it," I said and opened the door.

I try not to beat people over the head with my geek likes and tendencies, my love of comics and sci-fi and animation and the like. Not that I'm ashamed of it. But it can put people off a bit when you are all in their face about it. That can apply to anything, though. If you met some guy that was really into salsa and he was wearing a t-shirt and hat that said "I Love Salsa" and he was blaring salsa music from a boom box you would be like "Wow, this dude is REALLY into Salsa.... and he's freaking me out with it." I try not to be the salsa guy. I've seen enough comic geeks to know how well that can go.

So when you first enter my apartment, you're not assaulted by all things geek. Not at first anyway. The very first thing you may notice is that there is a Japanese movie poster for the original *Shaft* with Richard Roundtree, which is just to the left of the door, across from my coat closet. Black movie posters + Japanese design = badass. Every time. I have another Japanese movie poster of *Super Fly* in my bedroom, which isn't nearly as arrogant as it sounds. It was the only place left that had room. Seriously. There's also a *Godzilla Vs. Monster Zero* Japanese theatrical poster in there and a *Bullitt* Japanese one too. See? No huge ego. Although I'm sure some psychiatrist could write a paper on the Freudian overtones of those particular prints being near my bed. Hey, sometimes a poster is just a poster.

But the apartment does sort of become a shrine to geekdom when you fully enter it. The other framed pictures on the wall are all comic art and the entertainment unit that holds my television also holds about sixty or seventy different statues, action figures, toys and the like. Maybe eighty. Leaning against the unit on either side are my full size Captain America shield and Thor's hammer, Mjolnir, which cost me WAY too much money but were just too cool not to buy. A two-foot tall Godzilla (*Hensei* style for those in the know) guards the shield while a shiny Terminator and Striker Eureka from *Pacific Rim* keep their eyes on the hammer. I also had a few pieces of comic art framed and hung next to the entertainment unit, nothing even remotely like Coleman Chandler's collection but a few pieces that I loved and planned to never sell. Well, planned, anyway.

And that's just the start, really. Most of the people who visit me are geeks like me or just used to it. When I had new visitors who were not into all of it I became very aware of just how much stuff I have.

Jessica stepped to the middle of the room and stared at everything.

"Wow."

"Yep," I said, nodding.

Jessica blinked a few times and then shook her head.

"I give you credit, Will, you are a proud, not-messing-around geek." Then she frowned and peered at me intently. "Is it geek or is it nerd?"

"Geek," I said. "At least to me, anyway. Nerd is more math-y/science-y, I think. Like, if I were showing you my prized collection of moon rocks or some test tubes from

Thomas Edison's lab I would be a nerd."

"Ah. So, since you're just showing me framed comic art and statues of super-heroes you're just a geek." she said, teasingly.

I laughed and nodded slowly. "Yep. Yep, that's pretty much it."

"But I bet some of this stuff is valuable, right?" she asked, staring at Cap's shield. She turned to me and smiled. "Like, really valuable."

"Some of it probably is. I have some other stuff tucked away that could bring in some good money."

"Oooh, investments. Nice."

"I guess. Most of my stuff is of personal value to me. What I like."

She nodded and continued looking at the action figures and models and I continued looking at her. She was very, very attractive. I had to watch myself and not do something stupid.

"I'm sorry, I'm a lousy host, " I said. Come sit down. Would you like something to drink?"

"Um… water is fine," she said, distracted, and then picked up a phaser from *Star Trek VI,* the cool black and silver ones with the extra long "clip". She pointed it at me and said, "I like this one."

I put my hands up and got serious. "Be careful, Jessica.

That's set to kill."

Her eyes widened for a split second and then she smirked. "You jerk. You actually got me with that one."

I burst out laughing and retreated to the kitchen as she made "pew, pew" noises and fired at me. When I returned with her bottle of water she was posing with the phaser in two hands as she looked to the side, like she was peeking around a doorway. "Do I look dangerous?"

"You're too sexy to look dangerous." I said. That one got away from me but I couldn't help myself.

"You're cute." She smiled and took the water from me. Then she leaned in and kissed my cheek.

"But I can be both," she said in a low, sexy voice.

Jessica put the phaser down and backed up to the couch which faced the entertainment unit. Off to the right of the couch were two big windows and my prized Pottery Barn leather armchair in between them. I loved that chair. I got it at an estate sale and probably still paid too much for it but man, did I pass out in the thing occasionally. Worth it. The blinds and curtains were open so before Jessica sat down she looked out but besides the back of the building on 16th St. and a small alley there wasn't a whole lot to look at. She positioned herself on the couch and some pictures I had on a little table next to it caught her eye. One picture in particular made me groan inwardly.

"Are these your parents?" she asked, excited, picking up one. "This is a beautiful picture!"

It was. The two of them were bracketing me at my high school graduation, my mom looking proud and my dad looking proud but annoyed at the same time. He hated taking pictures. There were some more of them, like their wedding picture and one from when I was really small and we went to Florida.

"Yup, that's them."

"Look at you!" she laughed. "Where do your parents live?"

"Well, " I said. "They reside in Linden, New Jersey. But they don't "live" there."

Jessica stared at me for a second and then it dawned on here. "I'm sorry," she said.

"Like you said, it's not your fault. Or is it?"

She looked at me again although she was far more puzzled this time.

"Just repeating your line from earlier," I explained, sitting on the couch. "When we were looking at the big picture of your mom and your aunt."

"Oh, yes! Yes," She laughed and opened her water bottle. "Forgot about that. Wow. That seems so long ago for some reason."

"You're right, it does."

We were silent for a moment while she took a drink of water. I didn't know why it suddenly felt awkward.

"So," Jessica said. "Do you have any brothers and sisters?"

"Nope. Just me. Which was fine. Being an only child never bothered me. I did sometimes wonder what it would be like to have a brother or sister. I guess you didn't have to wonder, huh?"

Jessica rolled her eyes. "No, I knew all too well about having a sister. Ms. Goody Two Shoes."

"Your sister?'

Again, Jessica looked puzzled and then caught on. "Oh, no, I'm sorry. That's what she used to call me. Jennifer was always the black sheep of the family. Always getting into trouble. Drugs, police, stuff like that. Daddy kicked her out months ago. Took her out of his will. She hated me for being the "boring, do right" sister. Daddy's favorite." She shook her head and took another drink. "Family nonsense. You don't want to hear about that."

"I want to hear about whatever you want to tell me."

She smiled at looked again at the pictures. Then she reached over and picked up the one I was hoping she wouldn't.

"Who is this?" she asked.

The picture was of a young black lady, medium skin

color, with a beautiful full lipped smile and long black hair, her nose crinkled with laughter, her light eyes sparkly in the September sun of that day. She was wearing a salmon colored tank with an opened white button up blouse over it. She was quite lovely, stunning in fact. You couldn't see that she was wearing ripped jeans and sandals, her toenails a bright magenta. You couldn't see the tiny scar that she hated underneath her chin that she got when she was nine or the tiny tattoo of a bird on her ankle that got one night when she was drunk. And you couldn't see me, laughing as well, taking that picture and being happy that I got to take a picture of someone like her. I almost couldn't see it now, either. It seemed like another person got to take that in a different time, so long ago.

"That's… " I paused and then stopped. I genuinely didn't know how to answer the question. I guess her name would've been a good idea but I didn't even want to say it.

"Ohhhhhh," said Jessica. "The story."

I nodded.

"I won't ask what happened. Can I ask where she is?"

"You can ask," I said and shrugged. "I don't know. She could be in New York. She could be on Mars. God knows where."

Jessica looked at me, then the picture and then back at me.

“You obviously miss her tremendously. But maybe she’ll come back to you one day?”

I shook my head. “No. Sometimes things just don’t work out. No matter how badly you may want them to.”

"I'm sorry," she said and put the picture down. She was silent for a few seconds and then said, "Did I mention that you're cute?"

I laughed and she beamed at me.

"Ah, got you happy again."

"Just a ploy to make me smile, huh?" I said, giving an exaggerated pout. "You didn't even mean it."

Jessica slid closer to me and touched my leg. "I meant it. I think you are very handsome. Handsome and funny and very, very nice. I'm glad my father hired you. And I'm very sorry that someone hurt you."

I looked at her and smiled and realized that she was a lot closer to me than I thought. Her sky blue eyes were only inches from mine. I had never seen eyes that color that close. I could smell her perfume and feel the warmth of her hand on my leg and the next thing I knew we were kissing.

Her lips were soft and warm and then they parted slightly and I felt her tongue on mine. I touched her face with one hand and was just I starting to put my other hand around her when suddenly she was at the far end of the couch, her eyes wide and panicked.

"I'm sorry," I said, my hands raised. "I didn't...'

She waved me off and composed herself, "No. No. That was me. I just..." She paused and looked at the floor, thinking. I waited.

After a few seconds she said, "I'm... involved with someone. Seriously involved."

"Oh."

"At least I think it's serious. We've been together for a long time and it's.... it's not going anywhere. At least not where I want it to go."

'Marriage?"

"I'll take living together at this point," she said, standing. She turned and looked out the window at that crappy view but I'm sure she wasn't actually seeing it. "I'm sorry. I'm just frustrated with my relationship. I just want more of a commitment and I'm not getting it. I shouldn't be dragging you into it."

I stood too but I didn't approach. I didn't want to push up on her or anything while she was venting. "It's alright. I've been told I am a good listener."

"A good kisser too," she said and rolled her eyes. "There I go again."

"Well, I won't say I didn't like that part." I said. "Just being honest."

Jessica smiled at me and we just looked at each other for

a few seconds longer than we probably should have. Then she looked away and reassessed the apartment.

"This is, um... this is a nice little place you have here, Will. But where do you sleep? Does the couch pull out?"

"No, I have a bedroom," I pointed towards the front door but to the left of it. There was a short hallway that led to the bathroom but I could see how you wouldn't notice the bedroom, which was on the other side of the wall of the living room. "Over there."

"Oh!" said Jessica, surprised. "I thought you had a studio apartment." She walked to the hall, made the left and I heard her say "Nice." Then: "Oh, you have a cat?"

I followed her to the bedroom. Jessica was standing near the bed and Thor was spread out on her side, her paws out in front of her. She let out a yawn and considered Jessica's hand as it was carefully offered to her. Thor sniffed her, then licked Jessica's fingers and then rubbed her face against them. Attention whore.

"Aw, she's sweet," said Jessica. "What's her name?"

"Thor."

Jessica stopped rubbing and gave me a look.

"Thor? Seriously, Will? Does everything have to be geeked out?"

"No, there's a good reason. Really," I walked over to Jessica and pointed at Thor's head. "See how her face is all gray but the top of her head and ears are white? It's like she's wearing a winged helmet like Thor."

Jessica's face scrunched up. "Thor doesn't wear a helmet."

"No," I said, semi-annoyed. "That's movie Thor. Comic book Thor wears a helmet with white wings... well, he used to, anyway. Now he has the metal winged helmet but he used to have the helmet with the bird wings and why am I even attempting to explain this?"

She laughed and then picked up a trade paperback off of my nightstand that I had just gotten on eBay called *Silver Surfer: Requiem*. She flipped through it and said, "He's cool."

"The Surfer? Yeah. Are you familiar with him?"

She turned through a few more pages and then answered. "Yeah. Um... he was in that Fantastic Four movie."

"Where Galactus was a cloud," I shook my head. "Major point of contention with comic book fans."

"Yeah, isn't he supposed to be a giant guy? In a crazy helmet?"

That surprised me. "You don't know Thor's helmet but you know Galactus has one?" I laughed.

She turned a little red, shrugged and put the book back down. Then she turned her attention to the posters around the room. "*SuperFly*?" she said, eyebrows raised.

"Stop." I said, smiling.

She walked over to the wall opposite the bed where I had

original comic art framed and hung and pointed to an empty space between two of the pieces. "What happened here?"

"Yeah, I had to sell a piece. I needed the money."

"Oh, that's too bad. Was it a piece you liked?"

"One of my favorites," I said, standing next to her. "A Michael Golden page from *Doctor Strange* #55. Just a great piece, Sold it to this guy named Rich Cirillo. Rich is cool. He'll give it a good home."

Jessica snorted. "A good home? So he'll feed it and water it?"

"And take it out for walkies." I said and she burst out laughing. Then she turned, put her arms around me and kissed me deeply.

I held her and returned the kiss, feeling her body against mine and smelling that perfume again. Her hands slid under my shirt and up my back, her nails gently raking me. I fought back a shiver and held her tighter against me with one arm and ran my other hand through her hair. She made a very small sound deep in her throat, like a tiny moan and then pulled back slightly, her half lidded eyes staring into mine.

"Jessica," I whispered. "Your man…"

"Don't make me think." she breathed and kissed me again.

- - - - - - - - -

It was later when we were lying in my bed with me talking about her dad and Jessica listening. I had been holding her but then she very slowly pulled away. I really didn't think anything about it but then she abruptly got up, gathered her clothes and went into the bathroom. I heard the door close and then nothing.

I stayed there for a minute, on my back, looking up at the ceiling and then I put on my boxers and went to the door. I knocked lightly and waited.

"Jessica? You ok?"

Silence.

"Jess?"

The door opened and she was fully dressed except for her little jacket which was draped over the end of the bed. She hurriedly shouldered past me and turned into the bedroom, avoiding my eyes. I followed her and leaned against the doorjamb, watching her. She walked back and forth past the bed three times before she realized where her jacket was, then picked it up, aggravated.

"I have to go," she said, clumsily putting the jacket on.

"What's wrong?"

Still not looking at me, she fumbled for her bag. She searched through it, confirmed her phone was there and then put here arm through the tiny straps until they rested on her shoulder.

"Nothing. I just..."

I walked to her and gently put my hands on her upper arms. She jumped slightly and I felt terrible for startling her. What had just happened? I could feel tension tightening her whole body as she stood there stiffly. She still avoided my eyes and all I could see was the top of her head and blonde hair trailing downward.

"Did I do something wrong?" I asked. "Talk to me."

She shook here head, sighed and finally looked at me.

"We shouldn't have done that," she said.

It was my turn to sigh then. I let go of her arms and rubbed my eyes. "Jessica..."

"I'm not blaming you, Will. Not at all. This was my fault. I let this go too far," she shook her head. "It's completely my fault. I wanted this to be professional."

"It still can be," I said. "What happened here doesn't change that. Whatever we did or will do later won't change the fact that I am working for you and your dad and I am going to do my best job on this."

Jessica sighed again and walked past me and out into the living room. I followed.

"I hear what you're saying but... I am in a relationship and you're doing stuff for my dad... it just isn't right. I have to keep this straight, you know?" She walked over to me and took my hands. "You made me feel a way I haven't in a long time. You really did. But I can't go any further with this. And I need you to respect that."

I started to speak but really didn't know what to say. Jessica pulled her phone out of her bag and dialed a number. I heard my phone in the bedroom chime and vibrate.

"Yeah, that's me," she said. "I want you to call my cell directly with any info you have on the page. Anything. The number I called you from before is my dad's cell. He was sitting there when I first contacted you so I just ended up using his. But if you call him back on his phone you'll be lucky if he answers. Keep me up to date and I'll relay it to dad. As soon as you find that cover, call me."

"Ok."

"You saw my dad, how crazy he is about this art. I really, really want to find it for him, to make him happy. And I know you can."

I nodded. "I'll find it."

Jessica stared at the floor for a second and then looked at me.

"I'm sorry," she said. "I didn't mean for this to happen. There is definitely.... a thing there between us, Definitely. But I can't pursue it."

Once again she approached me put her hand on my face.

It was warm and soft and gentle.

"Tell me you understand. Please."

I did understand but didn't at the same time. If she wasn't happy with this guy she was with… but then I stopped and really looked at it. Who was a kidding? She was white and loaded. I wasn't destitute but I definitely couldn't run in her money circles. And working for her dad was one thing. I'm not sure how he would react to me getting up close and personal with his daughter. Maybe Jessica was right. This wouldn't work out one hundred times out of one hundred. I had to be realistic about this. We had two worlds colliding here. No matter how much I wanted to take it further it couldn't work.

But, damn, it seemed pretty good.

"I understand," I said. I'm sure I didn't sound very convincing.

"Find that page for my dad. And for me," She kissed me on the cheek and we looked in each other's eyes. "But pretend this didn't happen. I wish we didn't have to but please. Just pretend that these last few hours didn't occur, like it was a dream. It's better if we didn't speak on it. Ok?"

I shook my head slowly but said "Alright."

"And remember to call my cell."

"Ok."

We stood there and looked at each other and I didn't

know what to say. She looked like she didn't know what to say either. So we both stood there not saying anything until Jessica sighed again and adjusted her little bag on her shoulder.

"I'm sorry." she said again, walked to the door, opened it and stepped through. She closed it behind her softly, guarding against the slam. That was nice, at least.

I stood there and listened to her walk down the hall towards the elevator. It was quiet and I thought that maybe she would come back but there was a bing sound and then the elevator door sliding open. Then it closed and there was nothing.

I waited a few minutes, thinking maybe she would call or text or do something but she did none of those things and after a few more minutes I realized that I was standing by my front door waiting for something that wasn't going to happen.

I slunk over to the couch and sat heavily. It was amazingly quiet, way more quiet than Brooklyn at this time should be. I heard a Q train rumble to a stop at the Cortelyou Road station a few blocks away and then after half a minute it started back on it's journey out towards Coney Island. Then it was silent again. I looked at the picture of Her on the table and for about the billionth time I wondered where she was and how she was doing. Was she happy? Sad? Neither? Did someone that she liked just confuse the hell out of her and walked out of her place and left her feeling wistful? Or was that just me? Probably just me.

Thor sauntered over to me and meowed, her eyes big and black in the darkening room. She could read that I was feeling bluesy and out of sorts. Or at least, I liked to make myself think that she did. I let her jump on my lap and I sat there stroking her and listening to the low car and bus noises that I probably was just too fuzzy brained to hear before. Then, after sitting in the dark for God knows how long, I got up, ate some reheated Beef Lo Mein and went to bed.

5

It wasn't a good night of sleep. It probably should've been, all things considered, but nowhere near. Too many half formed dreams with people I didn't want to think about interacting with people I did. I must've woken up about a dozen times and in every one of those instances it felt like Thor was cutting off the blood flow to a different part of my body. Finally, after lying there and listening to Brooklyn shift from night noise to morning noise, I sat up in bed, annoying Thor enough to vacate my crotch area. I felt like crap, creaky and cranky but not sick. Just not all together. Maybe it was the lukewarm leftover Beef Lo Mein dinner. When in doubt, blame the old Beef Lo Mein.

It was 6:54 and there was no good reason at all for me to

be up then, certainly not to call people about a Superman cover. I slid out of bed, got a twenty ounce Pepsi from the fridge in the kitchen and came back to the bedroom. The cap twisted off with a satisfying hiss of carbonation and I took a happy sip. Pepsi is my main drug of choice. People love coffee but this was my jumpstarter, my engine in the a.m. I looked at the plastic bottle filled with dark goodness and said, "Only you understand me, my Brown Liquid Queen." Then I realized just how stupid that sounded and turned the TV and the PlayStation on. Nothing can get you back on track faster than a Pepsi and shooting people in *Call Of Duty*. I don't know how you would test for that but I'm pretty sure it's true.

It was after 9:30 when I decided that I had drank enough Pepsi and shot enough people - or in my case, got shot by enough people - so I fell back on the bed, reached for the phone and made a few calls but I came up empty. No one had any leads on the Swan page and stupid Donnie still hadn't texted me the dude in Jerseys' number. I damn sure wasn't going to call him back. I had my fill of that guy for the present.

After staring at the ceiling for a few minutes I got up and shuffled to the kitchen to feed Thor. She heard me opening the cupboard and was coiling around my ankles instantly, meowing. A little while back I was just some guy who aggravated her by waking her up. Now I was the dude keeping her from starving to death. Cats are funny. I mixed in a combination of dry and wet food and bet myself whether she would stay and eat it or turn her nose up and walk away. I took "turn her nose up" but Thor surprised me by digging in hungrily. Never fails. If you give me a 50/50 chance on getting something right I'll get it wrong 90% of the time.

While Thor gorged herself I filled her water bowl from a bottle of water in the fridge and headed to the bathroom. I still wasn't up to speed and I was hoping a good hot shower would do the job. Once in under the hot water I felt better. I soaked my head under the stream and stood there, letting it push every negative feeling out of me and down the drain. Never underestimate the power of a long, hot shower.

I was drying myself off when my cell rang in the bedroom. When I saw it was Donnie I rolled my eyes, sat down on the edge of the bed and answered it. So much for pushing away the negative feelings. I took a breath and answered.

"Hello?"

"Farrar! What's up?"

He sounded way too cheery and pleased. I actually thought it wasn't Donnie at first.

"I'm... good. What's happening? When can I get that

guy's number?"

"Yeah, I'll get that for you. Are you home?"

"Yeah."

"Ok. Listen, Farrar, I'm going to give you this guys number. But I want you to come up to the store. You're a man of your word so if you say you're gonna come up I know you will. I want you to see the store."

I sighed. This guy was driving me crazy about this damn store.

"Donnie, I will see the store soon. Just..."

"No, no, no, no, no. I want you to come up now. I want your word that you will come up now and check it out."

"So, you're holding this guys number hostage until I agree to come up there."

Donnie laughed. "No, it's not like that at all. Not really." He laughed again. "I just know that if you came up here, maybe posted about it on Facebook, I can get a little more business out of it. You know."

I put my head in my hand. This guy was unbelievable. I rarely posted on Facebook and now I had to do a fucking advertisement for him? I started to get mad but decided that it wouldn't be the end of the world and I could have five grand plus from Coleman Chandler to make me feel better about it.

"Fine. I just got out of the shower. I'll head up there now

since this is so Goddamn important to you."

"Great! Cool!" said Donnie, all pleased and completely ignoring my annoyance. "I'll text you that guys number then. Alright, man, I will see you soon!"

He hung up and I sat there for a few minutes trying to wrap my brain around Happy Donnie but it was like trying to understand quantum physics so I gave up. I stared at the wall for about five minutes, thinking about the Superman cover, Jessica, Donnie's annoying ass and about thirty other things and then I got dressed. The Weather Channel said it was a little cool so I grabbed a jacket out of the closet. Then I said bye to Thor and left.

Luckily it was too early for Pierre to be at his station because he would definitely have some wise guy comments about the day before. The early shift guy was Eddie, an older Puerto Rican man who was a big Mets fan. After crying on each other's shoulders for a few minutes I told Eddie goodbye and headed down the street to my Jeep. I was maybe twenty feet out of the building when my cell buzzed. The number wasn't familiar to me at all but maybe I had a new lead.

"Hello?" I said.

"William Farrar?"

"Speaking."

"We need to talk."

"We are talking."

The voice let out an annoyed huff of air and said, "In person, I mean."

I stopped walking and leaned against a mailbox. My Jeep sat right beyond it. "Well, who is this?"

The voice tried to sound threatening. "Don't worry about who this is. That's not your problem."

I laughed and said, "You're gonna have to do better than that to make me meet you."

There was a chuckle and then the voice said, "Turn around."

I looked behind me and saw a big, long haired guy wearing skinny jeans, a black tee and a long sleeve red and blue muted plaid shirt walking towards me, holding a phone to his ear. He had tiny eyes that seemed too close together and a big cartoon jaw that made him look like a bad guy from a Bugs Bunny cartoon. Chuck Jones would've loved this dude.

"Looks like we're meeting." he said.

Big guy. Long hair. Big jaw. Fucking Donnie, I thought. He was telling the truth.

Big Jaw Guy walked up to me and put his phone away. He looked past me and nodded so I turned around and there was a little rat-faced guy standing about two feet behind me. He too had on skinny jeans, a black tee and a plaid shirt but his was a darker blue with mint green highlights. He must've been about 5' 4" or 5' 5'" and real wiry looking. Nice, a team.

"Oh, so you guys are on some sort of cloak and dagger shit." I said. "Ok. So what's up?"

The little guy stayed behind me so I couldn't get both of them in my view at one time, which I didn't like. I angled towards the Jeep and leaned on it and that helped keep him on my side but I was still in a vulnerable spot. You always have to keep an eye on the little guys.

"My associate and I have learned that you were looking for an item that we are interested in obtaining for ourselves." said Big Jaw Guy in a movie mob guy sounding voice, like he had just watched a marathon of *The Sopranos* before he came over here. Actually he sounded more like Joe Mantegna's Fat Tony character from *The Simpsons*. I had to keep myself from laughing at the "My associate and I" part.

"And what is this item that I am supposedly looking for?"

Big Jaw Guy smirked. "Not supposedly. Definitely. And I think you know what item I am referring to."

"At any given time I'm looking for a lot of items," I said. "So I'm going to need you to be a little more specific."

"Stop fucking around," piped up little rat-faced guy. He had more of a high-pitched voice, real grating and heavily Brooklyn sounding. If Scorsese made a cartoon for Fox this is what it would've sounded like. "You know we mean the Superman cover."

There was no point in denying it so I said, "Ok, yes. I'm looking for that. So what does that have to do with you?"

"I told you," said Big Jaw Guy. "We want it."

I looked back and forth at the two. "No offense but you guys don't strike me as Silver Age Superman fans."

"Don't worry about what we look like. We want the page when you find it. It would be in your best interests to hand it over to us." Big Jaw Guy paused and put his right fist into his left hand, trying to look menacing. "We wouldn't want anything to happen to you and yours, right?"

I'd dealt with guys like this before. They wanted everybody to think that they were connected so they always floated some vague bullshit threats and notions to get you thinking that, when in reality they were just sniffing around the edges of it, like they had an uncle who knew a guy who knew a guy. I hate these wannabe Mafioso Goombah types. Hate 'em.

"Listen," I said, turning to face Big Jaw Guy squarely. "I don't know if this Bobby D and Pesci act you got going on puts a scare in other people but to me you guys are about as Mafia as Pinocchio. When I find that page I'm taking it to the guy that hired me. You want a comic page? Go shake down some other asshole."

Now, I wouldn't consider myself particularly tough but I wasn't in the mood for this nonsense. Where did these knuckleheads learn about the page and the fact that I was even looking for it? Was Rick behind it? I had to talk to Jessica about this.

I felt a sharp punch in my right kidney and then Little Rat Faced Guy was trying to grab me around the neck. That's what I get for not keeping an eye on him.

"Listen, you fuck..." he started and I swung my left elbow back and connected with what I had hoped would be his ribs but because of his height was probably more like his chest and Little Rat Faced Guy made a sound like "Hurrrfff" and let go. I had turned my head slightly to look over my left shoulder and when I looked back Big Jaw Guy was throwing a long, looping right at my face. But he threw it from somewhere on Church Ave. and I had enough time to twist away from his big haymaker. His fist glanced off of my left shoulder and continued swinging until it connected with the passenger side back window of the Jeep.

"Fuck!" yelled Big Jaw Guy and while he was fiddling with his hand I kicked him in the stomach. He stumbled back and couldn't seem to decide whether to see to his busted paw or his newly kicked gut so he just doubled over and groaned. Then Little Rat Face Guy was back on me punching and kicking and suddenly I heard a woman's voice yelling "Hey! Hey!"

We all froze and when I looked up I saw Karen Carter walking towards us holding two plastic bags filled with groceries. She yelled "Hey!" at us again and then turned towards our building and yelled, "Somebody call the police!"

Little Rat Face Guy hopped off of my back and shoved me against the Jeep. Then he collected Big Jaw Guy, who looked like he was about to throw up, and guided him past me and down the street in a crouched run that made them look like escaping chimps.

I started to go after them but Karen yelled, "Will, no!" and I stopped. She was probably right. It's not like I'm Jason Statham or somebody. I had been pretty lucky in that fight. Taking on two guys in the street would probably not be my smartest move. But I was seething, boiling with anger, and it took a lot to not chase them down. Assholes.

Karen ran up to me and put her grocery bags down on the sidewalk, making sure nothing spilled out.

"Are you alright?" she asked.

"I'm ok. Just pissed off."

Karen started dusting me off for no conceivable reason, focusing on my ass area which I was pretty certain didn't need dusting. I just let her, though. She probably saved me from a fresh set of bruises.

"Who the hell were those guys?"

I started to answer but just then a new looking black Mustang with red pin-striping and an old fashioned louvered back window jumped out of a parking spot about fifty feet ahead of us and tore off down the street. It barely braked at the stop sign on Dorchester Road, then rocketed across the intersection and was gone. I could still hear it roaring off for a few more seconds after that. I had to admit, it sounded pretty cool.

"Thank you, Karen," I said. "That was gonna get very ugly very quickly. Luckily you scared them off."

Karen stopped dusting my ass and said, "You're welcome, sexy. I can't have anybody pounding on my boyfriend like that." She laughed and then bent to retrieve her bags but when she straightened she had a serious look on her face.

"But that's what you get for messin' with them white girls." she said. Then she turned back towards our building and left.

6

I stood there few a few seconds and watched Karen go. She had a little extra sway to the strut. It was apparent that she enjoyed getting that little dig in there. Smartass.

I fished out my car keys and got in the Jeep, rolling down the windows. I couldn't believe that these two punks found me and actually tried to brace me for some comic book art. What the hell was going on?

My cell buzzed and I saw that Big Jaw Guy was calling me again. I answered and said, "Fuck you."

"You got lucky," said Big Jaw Guy in his stupid Fat Tony voice. "We weren't looking to hurt you but if you don't give us that cover we will. You and that lady and whoever you care about. So don't fuck with us."

I hung up and tossed the phone onto the passenger seat. This was unbelievable. No one would believe this dumb shit was actually happening. Except Donnie, that jackass. Then I remembered that I was supposed to be driving to his store. Screw THAT. I picked up the phone and called him and about a second before he answered I decided that I wasn't gonna give him the satisfaction of saying, "I told you so!" about Big Jaw Guy. No way. He wasn't going to hear about my little meeting.

Donnie still sounded happy when he answered, which made me even more annoyed. "Hey, Farrar. You on your way?"

"No. No, I am not on my way. Something came up. So it's gonna have to wait for awhile."

"Aw, shit, Farrar. Come on, you said…"

"Goddammit, Donnie, I am not coming up there today. So get off my fucking back. I am not coming up there and you are gonna text me that guy's Goddamn number or I will shit all over you on Facebook. Do you fucking understand me? Do you understand what I'm telling you?"

Out of the corner of my eye I saw two women across the street staring at me and that's when I realized I had been yelling. I rolled the windows up and leaned back in the seat, calming myself.

There was silence on Donnie's end for a second and then

he said, “Ok. I’m sorry man, I didn’t mean to get you upset. I’ll text the number and you can come up here whenever you’re ready.”

“Thank you,” I said and hung up, climbing out of the Jeep. I did not expect him to be so understanding. I actually felt a little guilty for unloading on him. Just a little.

When I got back upstairs and into my apartment I dialed the number Jessica had given me the night before and waited as it rang. When she answered, she sounded very tentative, like she really wasn't sure what I was calling to say.

"Hello?"

"Hi, Jessica. Listen, something strange happened and we have to talk about it."

There was a long pause on her end. "Will.... please. We spoke about this. I really need to keep this professional..."

"I'm not talking about that," I said, sitting down in my big Pottery Barn chair. My back still was a little sore where Rat Face Guy punched me and I rubbed it while leaning forward in my seat. "Two guys came to visit me today. They tried to shake me down for your father's Superman art."

"Wait, “ said Jessica, clearly confused. “What?"

"Donnie Castiglia told me a about a guy, some big guy, who came to his store and tried to brace him for the Superman art. I thought he was full of shit but this morning that guy and another tried it on me. And we scuffled a bit on the street."

"What?" said Jessica again, alarmed. "Are you alright? Who the hell were these guys?"

"I'm fine. And I don't know. But they knew who I was and what I was looking for. And only a few people would know that. Like Rick."

"Rick?" She sounded completely stunned by that. "You think Rick has something to do with this?"

"Well, I'm pretty sure he was listening in at the house yesterday when I was speaking to your father. Why would he need to be that nosy?"

"Listen. Rick is... well, Rick is Rick. But I really don't think he had anything to do with this. Why? He's gonna do all this to get a comic book cover?"

"Well, somebody did."

"True. But I just don't see how it benefits Rick. He's got everything he wants at the house. Why risk it for a Superman cover?"

I didn't have a real good answer to that so I just grunted.

"So these two guys just walk up to you on the street and start threatening you?" said Jessica.

"Well, it was pretty much right in front of my building so they knew where I live. And they called me first. Just to be sure it was me, I guess."

"They called you?"

"Yup."

"Give me that number."

I actually pulled the phone away from my face and looked at it for a second, like something weird had just come out of it.

"What? Why? What are you gonna do?"

"We know some people in the New York City police department. I'll see if they can find out some info."

"Huh. Ok. I'll text it to you then. But just find out info. Don't push it further. Or go all vigilante on me."

She laughed. "I promise I won't. Give me the number. Don't think anymore about it. I'll take care of it."

"Ok." I started to say how much I enjoyed her company the night before and how much I'd like for her to at least consider coming over again but I stopped myself. Professional. There was an awkward pause and she said, "So, when you get a chance. Just send me that number. Ok?"

"Ok. And I'll let you know about any new info on the cover. If I learn anything."

"Ok." She was quiet then and so was I. We had a great time the night before, talking and laughing, and now it was like an ordeal getting through a conversation.

"Um," she finally said. "I gotta take care of something so… I'll talk to you later, then."

"No problem. Bye." I said and hung up. I sighed and stared at the phone. This was how she wanted it so I had to just suck it up and go along. Even if I didn't like it. I found the number for Big Jaw Guy and forwarded it to Jessica. Then I went to the fridge and took another 20 ounce Pepsi out. As I was twisting the cap off my phone buzzed on the table in the living room and I thought it was her replying but it turned out to be Donnie with the name and number I needed. I thought he might drag it out a little longer so I was sort of surprised he sent it to me so fast. Ol' Donnie was full of surprises today.

The text had the name Michael Rothstein and gave his number, which had a Jersey area code. I tapped the number and listened to it ring. Michael Rothstein probably couldn't shed any more light on this but you never know. Any little bit would help. After the third ring it was answered.

"Hello?"

"Hi, is this Michael Rothstein?"

A hesitation. "Yes. Who's speaking, please?" He sounded very on guard and defensive.

"Hi, Michael, my name is William Farrar and I am a dealer in the original comic art field. I wanted to ask you some questions about a particular piece of art, if I could."

Rothstein grunted. "Let me guess. This is about the Swan Superman cover."

"Um... yeah. So you've definitely heard this song before."

"Yeah, it's gone platinum for me. I've never gotten so many questions about an item that I don't even own. You're the fourth person to call me about this."

The fourth? "Really? Who else contacted you?"

"Well, first it was that jerk.... do you know Donnie Castiglia?"

I laughed. "Yeah."

"Ok, then when I say "complete asshole" in regards to him you totally understand where I'm coming from. First it was him. He asked me a ton of questions about it, like, over and over. He was really getting on my nerves about it. Then the next day, like, I got another call about it."

"Was it a kinda Mafioso sounding dude?" I asked. "Like, almost comical in the accent?"

"Yeah," he said, laughing. "Cartoon Mobster. He was actually trying to lean on me over the phone. Said he would pay me a visit to convince me to hand it over. I was like, first of all, I don't have it. I've never seen it, I didn't know it was out there and if Poon says I have it he's a fucking liar. And I like Poon. But to tell the whole tri-state area that I have something that I don't is just not cool. I was like, go bother him. Do you know Poon? Ken Tang, I mean?"

"Yeah, I do." I said, smiling. I bet at this point his mother was the only one who called him Ken.

"Ok. So then I said to this guy, secondly, enjoy yourself trying to find me, dude. Nobody knows where I live. Only family and my bestest of friends. But nobody else. All my purchases go to a PO box or the Post Office. And there's like a million Michael Rothstein's in Jersey. So good luck with that, Al Capone."

I laughed. "Well, I'm glad you're actually taking the time to talk to me about it."

"You at least gave me your name. And while we were talking I Googled you. You have a web presence. People know you and apparently like you. So you I'll speak to you.'"

"People on the internet like me? I didn't think the internet knew who I was."

"Oh, it knows. Just don't let it know where you live."

I thought about my two buddies rolling up on me right outside my building and I could see where Rothstein was coming from. Probably too late to put the genie back in the bottle, though.

"So, what happened after you told him that?"

"Ah, he gave me some bullshit threat but it sounded kinda half-assed, like he believed me too."

"Ok," I said. "Now, you said you got another call."

"Yeah. That call was kinda weird, too. Some guy. Asked me pretty much the same things that Donnie did, like he was confirming. I think at first he might've thought I was lying about it, too. But I think I convinced him that I didn't have it."

So who was this now? Regardless of what Jessica had to say I still believed that musclehead Rick was up to something. I started to ask what the guy sounded like and then remembered that Rick never once said anything to me.

"And I suppose he never gave his name." I said.

"Nope. I asked him what his interest was and he said that he had heard about the cover and that I had it. I think Poon told half the planet I had it. So I told this guy like I told Donnie. Poon never sold me that art. I bought a Swan interior page and a Murphy Anderson cover from him. I definitely didn't buy that Swan cover. I probably would've if I knew about it but Poon never once said anything to me about it. I only bought those two I mentioned. I sent a copy of the receipt, because I want receipts for all of my purchases, to Donnie and I offered to send it to him but he told me it wasn't necessary."

"Hmm," I said. If one more person got involved with this I was going to need a scorecard.

"So I have a question for you, Will. Just what is the deal with this cover?"

"That is an excellent question, Michael."

"For which you do not have an excellent answer, I assume."

I blew air through my mouth and leaned back. My back was still sore but not as bad as before. "Nope."

"Is it signed, maybe? By Swan, or Leo Dorfman or George Klein, maybe?"

Now, I had to look up the issue on Comicvine.com to find out that Leo Dorfman wrote two of the stories in the comic and that George Klein inked the Swan story. I had a feeling that Rothstein knew that info like he knew his phone number.

"Not as far as I know. I mean, I wasn't told that. It's possible, I suppose. But that doesn't fully explain all the interest."

"Hmmmmm," said Rothstein and then he fell silent. Probably trying to think of the crazy loophole that made this cover so sought after. There was a commotion in the bedroom and Thor came bounding from that direction, slapping a balled up piece of paper across the floor. I had no idea where she had gotten it from. She stopped and looked at me for a second and then chased the paper into the kitchen. I heard her crash into her food bowl and shook my head. Oh well. She was being more productive than I was at the moment.

"Wait," said Rothstein. "Wait. Are you sure it's *Action Comics* 305? And not *Action Comics* 309? Are you sure?"

"Well, I was told 305. And the cover was described to me. When I looked up the issue that's I saw. Why? What's so special about issue 309?"

Rothstein chuckled.

"Oh, that's an interesting story. I'm surprised you've never heard about this."

"I'm dumb. Humor me."

He chuckled again and said, "No, you're not dumb. I know that. You just never heard it. Ok. This is back in late

'63. In the issue President Kennedy appears and poses as Clark Kent so that Superman can go save lives."

I laughed. "You have to love DC and their crazy imaginary stories back then."

"Yeah, they came up with some doozies. But this one almost bit them in the ass. Kennedy got assassinated about a week before the issue came out. It was too far along to stop distribution."

"Yikes."

"Yeah. I think most people at the time understood, though. It was too late, they couldn't have stopped it. So, as a result, original art from that issue has an elevated price tag. The cover recently sold for, like $110,000 or something like that."

"Double yikes."

"So I'm wondering if this is that cover. It's worth a lot of money. That would explain all the phone calls."

"But that doesn't make sense," I said. "He's asking me specifically for #305. If he wants the cover art for #309 I'm not gonna find it because that's not what he asked for. You know?"

I could hear the air go out of Rothstein's sails right through the phone. "I guess you're right," he said, sounding all dejected. "How could you find something that you're not looking for in the first place? Damn. I just wanted to make some sense of this."

"I hear ya. I do too. But I guess I won't know what the deal is until I find it."

"Yeah. Well, I know we just squashed the whole JFK theory but I'm gonna ask around anyway, see if I can find out where that art is. And please, when you do find out what's the story, let me know. I'm really curious."

"I will," I said. "And if you think of anything else that might be helpful text or call. I'm gonna need all the help I can get on this one."

Rothstein laughed and said he would and we hung up. I sat there and drank my Pepsi and rubbed my back and thought more about this nonsense that I was caught up in. Then, tiring of that, I looked at the cable box for the time. 12:15. Nice. I had woken up crazy early for no good reason, got into a street fight with some junior mobsters and then had a bunch of phone conversations that told me absolutely nothing. And all before lunch.

I got up and headed to the door, considering a hot plate of Orange Chicken and white rice from the Chinese restaurant. If no one else reached out to me I was done for the day.

7

If you ask any serious comic fan what the best day of the week is, they will say Wednesday. Why? Well, as you might already know or might have already guessed, Wednesday is new comics day. All across our great nation, in comic shops big and small, the hardcore reader, the casual fan, the just getting into comics (because of all the superhero movies), the getting back into comics after years away (because of the superhero movies), the parents buying for their kids, the parents buying with their kids and myself are all picking up whatever are their faves or whatever catches their eye. That can be a good amount of people so, once in a while, I will skip Wednesday and go Thursday, just to avoid all the different types of comic fans I just mentioned. Usually, though, I hit the shop around ten thirty on a Wednesday, nice and early. So after a pretty uneventful evening of Call of Duty, Chinese food, Pepsi and the New York Knicks (if they had won it would've been more eventful), I got up after a better night of sleep than the night before and hopped on the Q train towards Manhattan and Midtown Comics.

I frequent a couple of different stores in the city, like Jim Hanley's Universe on 32nd St and Forbidden Planet down on Broadway but I primarily buy my comics at Midtown on 40th and 7th which is, well, midtown. Once you get to $100 in purchases at Midtown you can get $20 worth of comics free in their Rewards Program. I don't do that all at once, though (I know people who have) so it takes a while to build up to my discount. But it's worth it once I get there. Nothing like going to the register with a stack of comics and finding out that they are pretty much free. Win.

I rode the Q to Times Square and walked through the maze of tunnels until I emerged right under the store on 40th street just west of seventh. This was the main reason way I didn't take the Jeep. Driving into the city can be a pain in the ass but parking in the city is two pains. Maybe three, depending on the time of day. So much easier sometimes to just leave the ride at home and use the subway. Especially if it puts you off right on the doorstep, practically.

It was only 10:35 but there were plenty of people on the

street. It is, after all, Manhattan. But it was still a lot less then it would be in two hours or so when the lunch crowds starting filling the streets, either looking to sit down and eat or grab a bite and hustle back to the job.

The entrance to Midtown Comics is on 40th St. and is a long narrow staircase up to the second floor of the building, which is really Midtown's first floor. That's actually another reason to get there at an off peak time. You can be standing there for a while as a row of slow buyers or tourists are taking their time coming down the steps. I remember waiting one time as this old man was gingerly heading down and then turning around to see about ten impatient comic fans behind me. Very impatient. Thought the old guy was gonna catch a beat down for a second.

Though you enter on 40th the store actually reaches the intersection and has big windows that face out onto the streets with giant reproductions of characters like Spiderman and Wolverine decorating them. They also have a third floor (well, second really. It's just on the third floor) that has toys and models and figures. It's actually a pretty good store. They have a sister store near Grand Central that I never go to because it's smaller and out of my way. Let the East Side people go there.

I jogged up that log flight of stairs to avoid meeting someone coming down and was about halfway up when I felt my phone vibrating in my pocket. I took it out and looked at it and saw that it was the number that Jessica said belonged to her dad. Probably looking for an update himself. Hmmm, what to say? Hi, sir! I've talked to a bunch of people who have no info, get into a fight with two unknown goons who are after the page too and slept with your daughter! Well, that's about it for now but I'll keep you posted! No. No, that probably wouldn't be wise. I scooted back down the stairs and tucked myself into a little nook next to the entrance of Midtown and answered.

"Hello?"

I was surprised to hear Jessica's voice. "Hi, Will, it's Jessica Chandler. Just wanted to see if you had made any progress with the cover search."

I guess Chandler was sitting there and Jessica was making the call for him. It didn't sound like I was on speaker but I decided to play along and give my report minus the dustup with the Wonder Twins. Not that there was a lot to report besides that.

"Hi, how are you?" I said. "Well, I spoke to Donnie and he told me that the cover was in the possession of a guy we both know named Ken Tong, Ken claims to have sold it to another guy named Michael Rothstein but Rothstein says that Ken is mistaken and that he never got the cover from him. I have a call in to Ken but he hasn't gotten back to me yet. I've also reached out to a lot of people I know but nothing from them yet, either. So it's at kind of a standstill right now. I'm going to try Ken again. He's definitely my best lead."

"Oh, ok. I will definitely tell my dad. It sounds like you've made a little progress, though."

"A little," I said and then thought back to the other night with Jessica in my bed. I knew she had a man but it felt really good between us. Too good to just not speak on it ever again. There was probably a better time to talk about it but I didn't know when that would be. No time like the present.

"Listen… I don't know if your dad is sitting right there or not but… I just wanted to say that I really enjoyed the time we spent together. I hope you did too. I'm sorry it got confusing for you but I'd like to see you again. Just to talk and sort it all out."

There was a really long pause, an uncomfortably long pause, and I instantly regretted what I said. I put my head in my hand and mentally kicked myself. Should've left it alone. Finally, Jessica spoke.

"I'm sorry but…. I really don't know what you mean."

Dammit. DAMN. IT. Why did I go there? I should've just kept my big mouth shut.

"You're right. Never mind. Keep it professional. Yes, ma'am." I probably sounded a lot angrier than I intended but I was mostly annoyed at myself.

"Will. Wait, I don't…"

"No. it's ok. It really is. It is better to keep this

professional and not complicate it with anything else. I understand. I will get back to you and your father as soon as anything breaks. Ok?"

"Um... alright," said Jessica. She sounded like she didn't know what to say so just settled on "Are you ok?"

"I'm fine. There's nothing wrong. I'm cool. I will let you know if anything comes up."

"Sure, that's fine," she said and she may or may not have been saying something else when I hung up. Whatever. She wanted professional. I was gonna be like EPMD and be *Strictly Business*.

I started back up the stairs and took my time. I didn't give a damn if somebody was coming down or not. They could wait. Then I stopped about halfway up and leaned against the wall, clearing my head. There was no sense in being annoyed about this and dragging it around all day. You could make yourself crazy trying to figure people out. Screw that. Just let it go and keep it moving.

When I finally entered I headed over to the comics. Practically the entire right side of the store has new and recent comics in a long wall rack that reaches back towards the stairs to the next floor. The rest of the floor is bookshelves with trade paperbacks and books of different genres (sci-fi, horror, fantasy), filed back issues and the sales counter. It's a real nice place with a nice atmosphere when it wasn't packed.

I was looking at the new issue of *Thor* by Jason Aarons and Esad Ribic and wishing it could somehow come out twice a month when somebody behind me said, "You still wearing that thing? When are you gonna learn?" I turned around and a guy named Eddie Rosario was standing there. Eddie is a tall, skinny Puerto Rican dude from the Bronx that I've known for years from conventions and small comic shows. Eddie has got to be in his mid-thirties but he still looked like a kid, what with his slight build and inability to grow any real facial hair. He was wearing baggy jeans, a red and blue checkered shirt over a gray tee and his ever-present Yankees jacket and cap. Like I said, Eddie is from the Bronx and I'm pretty sure that if you're Puerto Rican and from the Bronx, legally you have to be a Yankee Fan. It's probably not on the books but I'll bet it's a law. Eddie was pointing at the top of my head and I knew he was goofing on my Mets hat, as usual.

"You need to stop the Yankees hate and come over to a real team, man," he said.

"I don't hate the Yankees," I said. "I hate Yankee fans."

Eddie laughed. "Hey man, don't hate on us because we have 27 World Championships. What's that, like, fourteen times more than the Mets?"

I chuckled and shook my head. "I should've recorded that. So whenever somebody asks me why I hate Yankee fans I can just play that for 'em."

Eddie laughed again and gave me a bro hug. "What's up, man? Hey, I heard you were beating the bushes looking for some Superman art?"

Damn, I think everybody in the city heard about this.

"Yeah, that's been interesting, to say the least," I said and then I thought about what time it was. "What are you doing here so early? I thought you came here on your lunchtime?" I knew Eddie worked in the area, over on 7th and 36th as a graphic artist in the apparel industry.

"Got the day off today. But had some errands in the area. Thought I'd beat the rush and stop in early."

See? I'm not the only one.

Eddie picked up an issue of the newest incarnation of *Moon Knight* and started thumbing through it.

"How is this book? Are you reading it?"

"I love Warren Ellis so I am into it. It's kinda like *Global Frequency* where the stories are not really connected. They kinda share a similar theme. Like his short run on *Secret Avengers*. And that artist, Shalvey, is really growing on me."

Eddie nodded, looked for the first few issues and picked them up. "I'll check it out."

"Hey, how's Lillian?" I asked. That was Eddie's wife.

"She's very good, thank you," Eddie picked up an issue of *Daredevil* and then started back towards the DC titles so I followed. He stopped, thumbed through an Image comic called *The Mercenary Sea*, which I knew nothing about, put it on his growing stack of books and continued. "Starting to worry me, though. I'm getting those "I think I want another baby" vibes from her."

I laughed. Eddie had a cute little girl already who must've been about four. I couldn't imagine having one young child, let alone two.

"Oh boy."

"Yeah. I guess I wouldn't mind. You never think you're ready but you're only ready when you do it. If that makes sense."

I guess it did. When we got to the DC section I picked up an issue of *Superman Unchained* that I already had but hadn't gotten around to reading yet. Eddie was thumbing through a copy of *Wonder Woman*.

"So this Superman cover is valuable?" he asked.

I've known Eddie for a while so I was used to his rapid changes in subject. I've watched him confuse the hell out of a few people with that. But even still, I was momentarily puzzled. Then I caught on.

"Oh, the art, right. Not sure, actually. Everyone is acting like it is. You wouldn't believe what's been going on with this. It's crazy."

"What is it, a Neal Adams cover?"

"No, before Adams. Curt Swan. It's a nice cover and it's

Silver Age but everybody is mad amped about it."

"Maybe it's signed or something."

"Yeah, that's what somebody else said. I don't know. I know Poon saw it but I can't get in touch with him to ask if there was anything special about it."

Eddie got a serious look on his face and stared at me.

"What?" I asked.

"You didn't hear about Poon?" he asked quietly.

I actually got that burn in the pit of my stomach feeling that comes along when I know something really bad happened. I hate that feeling. It's always amazed me how human beings have physiological reactions to things and it's different for all of us. I steadied myself and said, "What happened?"

Eddie sighed and said, "Poon is dead."

I had prepared myself for bad news but I wasn't prepared for this. I leaned on one of the bookcases and blinked at Eddie for a good amount of time before I finally found the words.

"What happened?"

Eddie shook his head. "Apparently he fell out of one of the windows in his apartment. They think he was cleaning it. Ended up in an alley. The super found him the next day but he probably was instantly dead from the fall. He lived on the 4th floor."

Poon was dead. I couldn't believe it. It was like a really bad joke that I kept hoping Eddie was telling me but he wasn't joking. I get braced by two knuckleheads looking for a piece of art that Poon had in his possession and now I find out he's dead. Oh my God. Could it be just a coincidence? How many movies have I heard a character say "I don't like coincidences"?

"Do the pollce suspect.... are they investigating?" I asked.

"No. They just think he...." Eddie stopped and his eyes got big. "Wait. You think somebody pushed him?"

"No. Maybe. I don't know. I was just asking. I mean, he fell out of a window? How often does that happen?"

"Probably more than you think. But I don't think the cops suspect foul play," He stopped, looked up at the ceiling and sighed. "I can't believe I just said, "suspect foul play." But no, no one seems to think that. Poon's mom said it was an accident."

"Ok," I said and shut up about it. Maybe I was looking too deeply into this. Maybe it was just an accident. I needed to shift gears before I started freaking Eddie out.

"When was this?" I asked. "How did you hear about it?"

"This was, I guess, last Wednesday or Thursday. I called Poon on Sunday just to chat and his mother answered. Said she was trying to contact people he knew through his phone and answer as many calls as she could."

I had met Poon's mom at a couple of conventions. Poon

had a table out at a few of them and had been selling original art. His mom manned the table sometimes when he got food or strolled around looking at other dealers. She was a really sweet woman. This must've been devastating.

"I called Poon a couple of times over the last few days." I said.

"Yeah, she told me she would try to reach out to people she was familiar with who had called or texted. She probably hasn't gotten to you yet."

I turned to the racks and stared at the cover to an issue of *Black Science* without really seeing it and let out a long breath. "When is the funeral?"

Eddie shook his head. "She said it's just a family thing. Doesn't even want flowers sent."

"Jesus. I can't believe Poon's dead."

"Yeah, it's pretty fucked up," Eddie said and then we stood there for a moment in silence. Then he looked at his watch and jumped. "Oh shit, I gotta bounce. Yo, I'll let you know if I hear anything more, alright?"

I said ok and we bro-hugged before he hurried over to the register. No one was there so he got rung up fast, waved goodbye to me and was out the door.

There were only a handful of people in the store so it was pretty still except for the radio, which was tuned to Q104, a classic rock station. Creedence Clearwater Revival was on and John Fogerty was asking have you ever seen the rain. Yes, John, I believe I am somewhat familiar with rain. I picked up a few more books and wandered around some more but I was not into it. The only reason I kept shopping was because I didn't want to come back into the city anymore that week. So I got what I needed but my mind was elsewhere the entire time. Could Poon's death have nothing to do with this whole stupid fiasco? Maybe it didn't; maybe Poon accidentally fell out of his window while hanging some blinds or something and all of this was a side effect of people not being able to reach him. Or maybe the wrong people did reach him and this was the result. Either way it had become crazy, a simple comic page turning into the Maltese Falcon with me caught in the middle. And then I find out Poon is dead and suddenly the incident with the Mob Boys seemed a lot less goofy and a lot more dangerous. Where's Humphrey Bogart when you need him? I was thinking all this through when CCR's *Bad Moon Rising* came on and I knew that was my sign to get the hell out of there before I made myself crazy.

When I got back downstairs I wedged myself into that little space next to the entrance and dialed Poon's number. I knew that Eddie said he mother would probably get in touch with me but I had to say something beforehand and not wait for the poor woman to call me up to pass along my condolences.

Hearing Poon's brief "leave a message" speech fully

drove his death home for me. I would never hear his voice saying anything other than this recorded message ever again. He was a very cool guy, funny, easy to get along with. I found him to be an honest and upfront guy and those were the guys you wanted to deal with in any business. I just prayed that his death was an accident, a stupid pointless accident, and that no one took his life purposely. I didn't want to think about that possibly being true.

After the beep I paused for a second. I hadn't really thought of what I was going to say. Then I gathered my thoughts and spoke.

"Hi, Mrs. Tang. My name is William Farrar and I was a friend of Po... uh... your son. You probably don't remember me but we've met at a few conventions. Anyway, I just wanted to say that I just found out what happened and I wanted to pass along my condolences."

I stopped, caught myself before saying Poon again and continued. "Ken was a really, really good guy and he will be missed. I know I'll definitely miss him. If there is anything you need feel free to call me and I'll help you out. Please take care and you have my prayers and my best wishes."

I disconnected the call and then stood there awhile watching people go by. It was getting towards noon so the streets were filling up a bit, the tempo of people's walks getting a bit faster. It was a beautiful day, a little cool but sunny and cloudless. Poor Poon. Maybe where he was now was now was a lot better than this crazy planet. I could only hope.

Originally I planned to walk to 34th to catch the train back home but after the news Eddie gave me I really didn't feel like it. I couldn't shake the feeling that Poon was murdered and that this whole stupid thing had ramped up to be something really scary. I went back to the Q train the way I came and I was so preoccupied that I don't even remember the walk through the tunnels or the train ride home. I barely remembered to keep an eye out for my two new buddies when I got to my stop but they were nowhere to be seen. And luckily no one was at the front desk when I walked into my building because I really didn't feel like talking. I definitely wasn't up for any more of Karen's smartassery either. I lucked out, though, and made it upstairs and into my place without any interference.

The apartment was nice and cool and quiet when I came in. Mostly everybody in my building as it work at midday so it's always nice and still at that time. Just what I needed. I peeked in my bedroom and Thor was in her usual spot at the foot of the bed, her back to me. Then she leaned back, looked at me upside down and let out a little meow. So cute. I walked over and rubbed her little neck while she purred happily. Nothing like a pet to make you feel a little better.

I went into the kitchen and got a Pepsi out of the fridge and was just opening it when my cell rang. Another number

I didn't recognize. I sat in my favorite chair and wondered what kind of hilarity I would be in for with now. Yay. I was going to let it go to voicemail but hearing it now or hearing it later wouldn't really make a difference. So I leaned back, got comfortable and answered.

"Hello?"

A stern, older sounding voice said, "Is this William Farrar?" The voice had a familiar tone to it, not so much being a voice I recognized but a type that I've heard before. I couldn't place it, though.

"Speaking."

"Mr. Farrar, my name is Detective Tidyman with the New York City Police department."

I sat forward in my chair. Ah. THAT'S what that tone was. Cop.

"This is he."

"Hi, Mr. Farrar, um, we have a little case on our hands here and we have reason to believe you may be able to help us out with it a little."

Was this related to Poon's death? Maybe they had something. Maybe they DID suspect foul play, no matter how corny it sounded.

"Does this have to do with a guy named Po... ah, Ken Tang?" I asked. Dammit, the poor guy was dead and I still couldn't stop calling him Poon.

"Pua who?" said Tidyman, confused.

"No. I'm sorry, not Pua, it's a guy named Ken Tang. He was a friend of mine."

"No. I don't know who that is. There's no one with that name associated with this case. Not to my knowledge, anyway."

"Oh, ok," I said. There went that theory. "Well, what's this all about?"

"I'd rather not discuss it on the phone, actually. We were wondering, Mr. Farrar, if you could possibly come down to the precinct and talk to us. When you have time."

I love how the cops make it seem like you actually have a choice in these things. Like I was going to say "Hell, no. I got better things to do with my time." I like to think that I did have better things to do with my time but that would've been an amazingly stupid thing to say to the police so instead I said, "Sure. I have some time now. Where are you?"

"I'm at the 110th Precinct. The address is 9441 43rd Ave. in Elmhurst."

I sighed and went into the kitchen to get a pen and post it to write the address on.

"Problem?" asked Tidyman.

"Nope. None at all." I said. I got the address again from him and jotted it down. "Ok, I guess I can be there within the hour."

"Ok. Tell the desk sergeant you're here to see me on the 3rd Floor. See you soon."

I disconnected the call and looked up how to get to the 110th precinct. What was that all about? Was I in trouble? It didn't really sound like I was in trouble. It sounded like somebody was, though, and as long as it wasn't me, I was cool. But I was disappointed that it didn't have to do with Poon. Maybe I was wrong, maybe it was just a stupid accident. I felt a little guilty for trying to turn it into a whodunit when Poon just simply might have made a mistake and died. Poor guy.

I was thinking that through when Thor walked in and laid down in a rectangle of sunlight on the floor. She looked up at me, green eyes at half-mast.

"The cops want to talk to me." I said. "What's that all about?"

Thor yawned and then began to lick her side. She stopped, nibbled herself and then went back to licking.

I nodded my head, faux impressed. "Good point. I hadn't thought of that."

I got up, grabbed my keys and headed to the front door. I hated driving to Queens, mostly because I hate Queens, as any self-respecting Brooklynite would. All those stupid confusing addresses. 115-45th Street. Then Road. Then Avenue. What the hell? Better to leave now. When I looked back at Thor she had her right hind leg pointed straight up in the air and she was licking her ass.

"See, now you're just showing off." I said and left.

8

The 110th Precinct was a three storied red brick building with a big wooden archway door that sat smack dab in the middle of 43rd Ave between 95th and 96th Streets in Elmhurst, completely bookended by private homes. The first floor was all done in beige stone, with a beige brick design decorating the corners of the building all the way to the flat roof where an old style stone cornice of the same color hung along it's length. Connected to the left end of the building was a one-story garage with two blue doors, one open to the dark inside. Blue and whites and other non-police vehicles were parked with their backs to the building, but it was a wide street so no one would be plowing into the oddly parked cars – hopefully. It was clearly an old building but it didn't look too bad. It wasn't the pre-war battle scarred fortress-looking dump I was expecting. I wouldn't call it inviting but I didn't run off screaming either.

I parked across the street and went through the arched entrance with the traditional green police station lights on either side. The inside of the building didn't look bad either, ancient but taken care of. Just like in an old time police station the desk sergeant sat high, looking down at those who entered. He had a round, emotionless face with small dark eyes, a downturned mouth and an impressively large nose. From what I could see of him, the rest of him was round too. He stared down at me and waited, looking annoyed about something. Maybe that was how he always looked.

"I'm here to see Detective Tidyman?" I said.

He continued to stare at me for a second as if he hadn't heard me and then said in an almost robotic voice "Third floor. Elevator is over there." He pointed to his right at the clearly marked elevator. You'd have to be blind not to see it. But I can imagine how many people asked him where it was. No wonder he looked annoyed.

"Thanks." I said and I thought of Clarence Boddicker, the character played by Kurtwood Smith in *Robocop.* After Robocop beats and arrests Boddicker he drags him to the station house and leaves him with the desk sergeant. Then

RB leaves. Boddicker looks at all the cops staring him down, spits a wad of blood on the blotter and says, "Just give me my fucking phone call." I love that line. It always makes me laugh. But since the desk sergeant probably wouldn't think it was funny and I like my brains on the inside of my head I kept it to myself. So I just rang for the elevator and rode up to three.

The third floor was one big room with a bunch of desks and cops either on the phone or typing or bullshitting. All four walls had windows and since a lot of the neighborhood was residential you could see above the houses for a good ways. Off to my left I could see LaGuardia Airport in the distance and a jet heading in for a landing. There was a cop sitting at a desk near the elevator and I asked for Tidyman. He pointed to another desk by a window where two men sat and yelled out "Ernie. Visitor." One of the men at the desk waved me over.

I walked over and the guy who had motioned for me rose. He was older, stocky, probably on the force forever. He looked haggard, his old blue suit sort of wrinkled and hanging off of him. He had a long face, the bottom half already green with shadow. His eyes were a dull brown behind the small glasses he wore which really was funny when compared to the big and wild black eyebrows that hung over them. They looked alive, like they were ready to crawl around his face. His salt and pepper hair just seem to lie down on his head. Everything on him looked tired.

The other guy didn't rise. He was black, medium complexion, bald-headed, smooth shaven and much younger. You could tell that he worked out. His neck and shoulders were big and his black suit jacket stretched around his biceps. The first cop was straight up old school. The only thing he might use weights for was to put on a guys chest while he questioned him. The older one nodded at me and extended a hand.

"Thanks for coming in, Mr. Farrar. I'm Detective Tidyman, this is Detective Himes." He motioned to the seat across the battered, dirty desk from him. "Water? Anything?"

"No, no," I said, sitting. I'd sat on more comfortable rocks. "I'm good. Just curious as to how I can help you." I looked at the desk next to me and some disheveled white guy with a bloody bandage on his head was manacled to a metal loop in the floor. He sat slumped in his chair, fast asleep. I could hear him snoring. He was alone at the desk and looked like he had been for a while. Tidyman looked at manacled guy and then shook his head at me.

"Don't mind him. He's had a rough day."

"Oh, ok." I said.

Tidyman sat and leaned forward with his elbows on the

desk.

"Well, Will… can I call you Will?"

I nodded.

"Well, Will, we were wondering if you could talk to us about Tommy Castiglia."

Tommy? "Do you mean Donnie Castiglia? I know a Donnie Castiglia."

Tidyman picked up a bottle of Poland Spring from the desk and unscrewed the cap. He took a swig of water.

"Nope, Tommy. He's Donnie's cousin. We spoke to Donnie already."

"Oh. Ok," I thought back. I couldn't remember ever meeting Donnie's cousin. "I don't know him, I don't think."

"No? He called you yesterday. Twice."

"Me?" I asked. "Donnie's cousin called me?"

"Seems that way," said Himes, casually. "You don't remember talking to him? Maybe he left a message?"

"No, I didn't have any messages yesterday." I wracked my brain trying to remember me ever having a conversation with Donnie's cousin or any member of his family for that matter. I drew a complete blank. They had to be mistaken. "Maybe he just hung up. Are you sure he called me?"

"Yup." Said Tidyman, after another drink. He pushed a sheet of paper across the table at me. It said Garmin across the top and looked like a series of directions. "He also visited you according to his GPS. You live at 400 East 17th, right?"

I looked at the sheet. Sure enough my address was listed as a final destination in the directions. I caught a quick glimpse of the origin point being 2792 East 27th St. in Sheepshead Bay. Now I was completely confused. I had never heard of Donnie's cousin and now he was supposed to have called me and visited me? I shook my head.

"I'm sorry but I don't recall ever meeting or talking to Donnie's cousin. I think you may have the wrong guy."

Tidyman reached under his desk blotter and took out a photo. "Let's try a different approach," he said and slid the picture to me. He raised the bottle to his lips and looked at me as he drank.

My blood froze, then boiled. It was a mug shot of a face that I wanted to see again, only with my foot stepping on it. He had the same stupid half smile and that same dumb long hair. It was the asshole that accosted me in the street the day before. I couldn't believe what I was seeing.

"This is Donnie's cousin?" I asked.

Tidyman nodded, watching me closely. I gritted my teeth and felt my face get hot. Donnie, you stupid fat fuck. You sicced your cousin on me. I was enraged. I told myself that when I walked out of there I was going to drive to Williamsburg and beat the fucking shit out of that motherfucker. I was gonna kick his fat, sweaty ass all over his bullshit comic store. I must've been way off in "Seriously Fuck Donnie's Shit Up Land" because I vaguely heard talking and it didn't occur to me that I was being asked a question.

"You had no idea?" asked Himes again.

"No." I shook my head angrily. "I didn't know who he was. He and some little pipsqueak fuck stopped me in the street near my place."

Tidyman reached under the blotter, came out with another mug shot and slid it at me. "Probably this guy. Mike Petricelli." he said. I picked it up and yeah, there he was, the stupid looking rat-faced bitch. I nodded.

"NOW I know who you're talking about. Assholes," Then I caught myself. "I mean, these guys are the assholes, not… not you."

"Gotcha," said Tidyman. "And "assholes" would be the general consensus on these two. So, what? You guys had a problem?"

I stared at the pictures and got even angrier. Stupid looking fucks. I wanted to run Mullet and his midget friend over. I threw the mug shots onto the desk and leaned back in my seat.

"Yeah, they were trying to brace me into giving a comic book page to them. Long story."

Tidyman and Himes both frowned and looked at me like I just said I was from Krypton.

"A... comic book page? Is that what you said?" asked Himes.

"Yeah." I shook my head. They clearly didn't understand. "Not like a printed comic page, like ripped out of a book. An original piece of comic art, the one they send to the printer. Penciled, inked, sometimes lettered. That's what I do. I buy and sell original comic art."

Himes leaned forward, brightening. "No shit? That's cool! Like you have Batman and Avengers original pages? Shit like that?"

"Calm down, nerd." said Tidyman, smirking. "Fucking geek." Then to me: "See, you got him going."

Himes laughed. "Yeah, man! Geeks are cool now, don'tchu know? So..." he turned back to me. "You can make money off these pages? They can go for a lot?"

"Oh, yeah," I said. "Depending on the year and artist and character it can be big money."

"Really?" said Tidyman, drinking again. "And how much would the page that your two buddies threatened you over go for?"

I suddenly felt really uncomfortable with where this conversation was going. I didn't know why. But suddenly I had the feeling like I was throwing a lot of information out there without knowing what the deal was. What had these assholes done? And how was I involved? I really didn't like knowing how my name got tied up in whatever nonsense these two had gotten into.

"Well, I don't know, really. I don't have the page. I'm still trying to find it. And they didn't threaten me, really. I mean, I never felt in danger. They were just, you know, trying to suggest... you know, like "Come on, man, we want first dibs." And I was like, "Nah, man, it's for somebody else. Get out of here." I laughed weakly. "It was really nothing."

Tidyman and Himes just looked at me. Tidyman took another drink from his water bottle and swallowed loudly. I could still hear the chained up guy at the other desk lightly snoring but I was suddenly aware that it was very quiet otherwise, very still. I was also aware that I just told a really lame lie.

"You know?" I said.

Neither detective responded for a second and then Tidyman slowly nodded. Another sip of water. "But how much would you say?" he asked.

"Um.... It could be two grand. It could be ten, maybe more. I really don't know, to be honest."

Both men's eyebrows went up, Tidyman's black caterpillars threatening to climb to the top of his head.

"Ten grand." said Tidyman.

"Yeah, but I don't really know. It could be a lot less."

Quiet again. I was really feeling uneasy, sitting on that hard ass chair in a police station with two detectives staring at me and more going on than I knew. I needed to steer this talk towards me getting some info.

"So, I don't know what's going on but these guys are definite fuck-ups," I said. "I can see them getting themselves jammed up. What did they do?"

"Do?" chuckled Tidyman. He took a last drink from his bottle and tossed it at the garbage can next to his desk. The bottle hit the rim, threatened to bounce out but finally fell in.

"They died." said Tidyman.

I'm not sure how many times I blinked at them before I spoke but it must've been a lot. I was certain I hadn't heard him right.

"Died?" I finally got out. "Did you say, "Died"?"

"Yep. Both of them. Shot in the back of the head. Twice. Found them in the front seat of Castiglia's Mustang over by the airport." Tidyman jerked a thumb behind him and almost on cue a jet rose from behind some houses in the distance.

"Wait." I said. I really was having a hard time understanding this. I just found out that Poon was dead and now I hear that the two dumb bastards that I thought may have something to do with it got smoked themselves. What the hell? “Wait. You’re saying somebody shot them both?”

“Yep. Those backseat drivers can be murder.” said Himes with a nasty smile.

Tidyman looked at Himes, shook his head, sighed and turned back to me. “You gotta forgive him, he just made detective.” He leaned forward and crossed his arms on the desk. “So, Will. Tell us more about this disagreement you had with these two.”

I was still getting over the fact that two knuckleheads that I had a beef with a couple of days ago had been shot to death. That was still rattling around in my brain and this guy wanted to talk about some stupid comic page we were fighting about? I couldn’t believe he was asking me that.

“What? Who cares about that?” I said, annoyed. “That’s not important. They’re dead. Do you have any idea who killed them?”

Tidyman chuckled and then smirked. It was completely without humor.

“Well, Will, if we knew that,” he said, “you probably wouldn’t be sitting here, right?”

Then it finally dawned on me. Ok, I’m stupid. Forgive me. But I didn’t have much previous experience with being a suspect in a double homicide. I stared at the two detectives for a few seconds, feeling an icy sensation wash over me.

“You think I killed them?” I asked quietly. I didn’t want

to ask it but I did.

"I'm not thinking anything yet." Said Tidyman. "This is what we do. We talk to people, get stories, check to see if people are lying to us and piece it all together. These guys ran with a lot of different people and pissed most of them off. So this is just the beginning stages. So. Did you kill them?"

I almost fell out of my chair. "What? No! Of course not."

Tidyman smiled and gave a little shrug. "One day that's gonna work. I was hoping you'd make my job easier. Save me some time. Now we gotta do it the hard way." He tapped on the desk a few times and sighed. "Ok. Where were you last night between 11:30 and 3:15 a. m.?"

"I was at home."

"Anybody with you?"

"No. No, I was alone."

"And no one can verify that?"

"Not unless you consider my cat a good witness."

Tidyman shook his head at me and smiled. "No, we find that pets do not make very reliable alibis."

I was starting to get a little panicky. This couldn't possibly be happening. Two knuckleheads that I had a fight with were dead and I had no alibi. They couldn't possibly think I did this. Could they?

"I mean, my doorman saw me earlier but he leaves

around 11:00 at night," I said.

Himes put on an impressed face. "Doorman. Nice."

"It's a co-op," I said. "They really want to keep the building nice."

"Security cameras?" asked Tidyman.

That was a good question. That could save me ass. "I don't know. I could check."

Tidyman waved a hand at me. "Don't worry about it. How about this. Where were you around 7 o'clock last night?"

I frowned. Seven o'clock? I thought for a second and then it came back to me. "Oh, that's pretty much when I went out to get some food. There's a Chinese restaurant around the corner from me. That's when my doorman saw me. We talked for about five minutes when I came back and then I went upstairs to watch the Knicks."

"So you went out at seven and how long were you gone?"

I shrugged. "I don't know, 15 minutes maybe. If that long. And after that I talked to the doorman and then I went to my apartment."

"And stayed."

"Yes."

"And watched the Knicks."

"Yes."

"Did they win?"

I laughed. "Uh, no. Got blown out. Bad season."

Tidyman shook his head. "I haven't paid attention to the Knicks since Red Holtzman left."

"Ok." I said. Then there was an odd little lull in the conversation. I looked back and forth at Tidyman and Himes and said, "So what happened at seven?"

Tidyman looked over at Himes and the younger detective picked up yet another sheet of paper from the desk and studied it.

"At 7:04 P.M. Tommy received a phone call on his cell from a phone belonging to a Miss Freema Patel of the Bronx. He received another two calls from this phone, one at 9:45 and the other at 11:10. After the 9:45 call Tommy plotted out another trip on his Garmin, this one being to the approximate location of where he and his boy were found shot to death."

I was completely confused now. "Who's Freema Patel?"

Himes put the sheet of paper down and smiled. "Freema Patel works for the Lakeland Bus Line at the Port Authority. Ms. Patel and a couple of her co-workers were in a Starbucks on 39th and 8th in the city when she realized that her phone had been stolen from her purse. She said she had it when she walked in. This was about seven. She reported it to AT&T with a friends phone but that just gets you a replacement phone. The phone company is just gonna write off the calls made after a theft report generally, unless they think you're screwing with them. It's a good way to set up a double-homicide."

"Can't you track stolen phones now?" I asked.

Tidyman chimed in. "Yeah, Apple and some of the other companies can track 'em.... if they're on. We've learned that if you turn the phone off immediately and use it briefly that negates the whole thing."

"Nice." I said.

"So, like I said," Tidyman continued. "Leads. Just following leads. We'll do some more digging. I'm sure your story will check out. And we have more to follow up on. You may not believe this but these two have managed to piss off more than a few people."

"I. Am. Stunned." I said.

"I'm sure. Imagine our surprise, as well. So, Himes and I are not clear on something here. You obviously know Donnie Castilgia. What does he have to do with this?"

I sighed. "The guy that hired me initially hired Donnie to find this cover art. But Donnie being Donnie, he decided that this art was worth more then he was getting. So he tried to squeeze some more money out of my client. This, of course, got him shitcanned."

"Ohhh," said Himes. "So Donnie hears you're on the case

now and gets his cousin-"

"Literally, his *cugine*." interjected Tidyman.

"-to try to punk you out for the page, knowing you wouldn't know who he was. Got it."

"Yeah," I said. I got angry again thinking about it.

"Ok, that answers that then," said Tidyman. "Oh, one more thing. I know this little squabble took place in the street so there are countless witnesses but did you specifically tell anyone about this incident? Anyone who might've known who these two goumba's were and might've wanted to do something about it?"

I thought back to me calling Jessica and telling her about what happened. Giving her the phone number that Tommy had used.

Don't think anymore about it. I'll take care of it.

"No," I said.

Tidyman and Himes both looked at me for a second, Tidyman's funny caterpillar brows climbing up his forehead.

"You sure?"

"I'm sure. I didn't talk about this to anyone else." Jessica couldn't have anything to do with this. I couldn't see that.

"Alright." said Tidyman and the three of us sat there in silence for a few seconds. Then Tidyman did a little drumroll on the desktop and leaned back.

"Well, I guess that's it, then. We may call you back if

anything pops up." He opened a side drawer and took out two business cards. "Mine and his," he said, jerking a thumb at Himes as he slid them to me. "You think of anything else, you call us."

"Ok," I said and stood. I was putting the cards in my wallet when prisoner guy at the next desk raised his head slightly, mumbled something and then dropped it again. He never even opened his eyes. Poor bastard. He was probably half-asleep, half concussed. Ascussed. I was pretty sure that wasn't a word but it should've been.

"We probably will have to talk to your boy Donnie again," said Tidyman. "His cousin Tommy might've been involved in a different type of family, if you get my meaning."

"Oh, great."

I couldn't see Tommy and his shithead friend being nothing more than flunkies in the Mafioso hierarchy but what do I know? Maybe they were more connected than they looked. Great, just what I needed. Some more Sonny Corleone types coming to visit me.

"Speaking of Donnie," said Tidyman casually but not casually enough for me to not realize this was why he mentioned that fat bastard in the first place. "I know you're a little pissed at him."

"A little."

"Understandable. But don't leave here and go do something stupid, Farrar. You hear me?"

"Gotcha. I won't do anything stupid."

Then I left, got in my car and went to go do something stupid.

9

I've lived in Brooklyn my entire life and in at least six different neighborhoods but I have to admit, I know almost nothing about Williamsburg. I know where it is. Williamsburg lies almost at the top of Brooklyn with only Greenpoint separating it from Queens and the East River separating it from Manhattan. I know that I've only been there a handful of times, the last one about five years ago at a party thrown by a friend of a friend of a friend. I know that like a lot of Brooklyn in the seventies and eighties, Williamsburg was a desolate, impoverished neighborhood. Lots of crime, lots of drugs. Well, like lots of Brooklyn back then. But eventually it's proximity to Manhattan led to re-gentrification by white hipsters and artists and musicians and Williamsburg was reborn as another over-priced neighborhood with a great view of the city. Actually, there was one last thing I knew about Williamsburg. I knew that I was going tear the whole fucking place down to get my hands on Donnie Castiglia.

Blastaar Comics was wedged between a health food store and a pharmacy on Lee Avenue, a stones throw away from the Brooklyn Queens Expressway. I found a spot in front of the pharmacy, got out of the jeep and stared up at Donnie's sign. On it, the Marvel Comics villain Blastaar was shooting energy beams out of his hands, as he was prone to do, at the store name, which was written in a dynamic comic font and was a vivid red and yellow. Blastaar was a big, stocky gray colored villain with a long gray beard and matching mane of hair. Donnie looked just like him, down to the big, ugly mouth and ape-like face. But unless Donnie had suddenly started shooting power beams from his fingers, he was gonna be ass out when I caught up to him.

I stormed through the front door, startling a skinny white kid behind the counter wearing an Adventure Time t-shirt. There were two adult customers thumbing through comics and a couple of kids sitting at a table with a bunch of *Magic: The Gathering* cards in front of them. They all looked at me like I was about to shoot the place up.

"Donnie," I growled and Adventure Time kid pointed at

the back of the store, where there was a door marked "Office". I must've had a crazy look in my eye because he didn't try to stop me when I walked past him, past the comic racks and tables and shoved open the door to the back room.

Donnie was sitting with his face in his hands at a desk with a computer and a printer and about a million pieces of paper on it. Comics too. And food wrappers. And soda bottles. If I didn't see the table legs I would've thought all of that mess was floating. The top of the desk was completely obscured. The rest of the office was about as neatly kept as the desk. There were stacks of books and unopened action figure boxes and display units and standees and all manner of crap. It was an absolute dump. I don't know how he kept track of anything.

It finally occurred to Donnie that someone had just burst into the room and he slowly raised his head and peered at me. His eyes were red from crying and he looked really tired and worn, his gray stringy hair limp against his head. I don't think he realized it was me but when I started moving towards him recognition dawned on his face and he started sliding backwards.

"No, no, wait..." he got out before I reached him and put a solid right into his face. The punch and his backwards momentum sent him and the big leather chair he was sitting in back and over. He crashed into a filing cabinet behind him and scrambled to get up, arms flailing and fat legs not seeming to work correctly. He looked like a drunken elephant. I was on him immediately, grabbing his old, dirty *Kingdom Come* Superman shirt while he was still on his knees. His hands flew up to protect his face and I hit him again but in the belly this time. It was like punching a sack full of wet blankets. He let out a loud "HAAARUFFF." and threw his arms around his midsection while I stepped back in case he upchucked. If he threw up on me I would've burned his fucking store down. That would've been the last straw.

"You stupid fuck, " I said. "I oughtta kick your fat ass all over this store. I can't believe you did that." That's what I said but I could totally believe it. It was so Donnie-like I was actually annoyed at myself for not figuring it out before.

Donnie was on his hands and knees looking down at the floor and he started crying and saying stuff that I couldn't make out through all the blubbering. The kid in the Adventure Time shirt tentatively stuck his head through the door and I said, "Get the fuck out."

"Ok," he said and left.

"You killed him," said Donnie, finally making sense. "You killed my cousin."

"What?" It took all my strength not to kick him in his face. "I killed him? I didn't even know he was your cousin. I didn't know who the hell he was. How would I have killed him? YOU got his ass shot, not me, with your stupid bullshit. That was YOU."

And I guess deep down inside Donnie agreed with me because he started crying harder than ever. His back heaved as he bawled and he took in loud lungfuls of air, like it was really hard to do. I thought he was hyperventilating and started to get a little worried. I didn't need this guy ending up in the hospital after I had pounded on him. I had enough problems.

Donnie seemed to get his breathing under control but he was still crying pretty good. Then he looked up at me, like he was pleading to take back what I said. Dammit. I wanted to stay furious at him but seeing him on his knees with tears running down his face and with this look of complete anguish made it almost impossible. It was a pretty pitiful sight. I mean, I was still mad but I didn't want to beat his brains in anymore. And I actually was starting to feel bad that I suggested that he got his cuz blasted.

"Listen,' I said. "Listen. Tommy getting killed probably had nothing to do with this. This cop I was talking to said that he and that other dude had pissed off a bunch of people. Probably somebody with a much better reason to kill him did it. It wasn't me and it wasn't you. Ok?"

Donnie got up slowly, turned his chair upright and finally, after enormous effort, got himself into it. I got winded just watching him. He wiped his face with his shirt and then put his head down on his desk and then tried to compose himself. I waited.

Adventure Time kid from the front stuck his head in again, keeping a close eye on me. In fact, he never looked away from me and he hugged the door tight, like he would slam it shut and run if I came at him.

"He's ok," I said but the kid didn't look like he believed me. I guess I couldn't blame him.

"Should I call the police, Donnie?" he asked. He really looked like he was going to run now. Donnie wiped his face again with his shirt and cleared his throat but he didn't lift his head.

"No, don't call 'em. I'm ok. Nothing to worry about."

"Ok," said the kid but he still looked at me like I was a supervillain. All of a sudden this little dude was hard. He never took his even stare off of me while he slowly closed the door. Hmm. Maybe I should leave by the back way. This skinny little geek was weirding me out.

I was still looking at the door when Donnie said, "You're wrong."

"'What?"

He still was looking down at the desk but his voice sounded stronger. "Tommy dying has everything to do with this. And that old man and his bitch daughter are responsible. I know they are."

"Whoa," I said. What the hell was this guy talking about? "Whoa. That doesn't even make any fucking sense, Donnie. They just want the cover. That's all. They're some rich white folks who live in a nice neighborhood and drive expensive cars and shit. They don't go around cappin' motherfuckas in the dome on some deserted street on the ass end of Queens."

Donnie finally looked at me. His eyes were red but hard; he was well on his way to being his old asshole self again.

"Yeah, they don't do it. They hire other people to do it."

I laughed and leaned against the door, hoping that kid didn't come back. He would probably shit himself if he tried the door and it wouldn't budge.

"Now you're just talking crazy," I said. "How would they even know who your cousin was?" I remembered that I gave Jessica the number that Tommy called me from but decided to keep that to myself. No sense in adding fuel to this fire. Besides, I had already talked myself into thinking that she couldn't have anything to do with this. How could that be?

"I don't know how they found out but they did," said Donnie. "And I found out earlier today that Poon is dead. Why didn't you tell me?"

"I just found that out, like, a few hours ago, Donnie. That was an accident."

Donnie got up from his chair and started straightening his desk up but was really just moving stuff from one side to the other. Busy work.

"Yeah, ok. It's just a big ol' fuckin' coincidence that the guy who actually had the cover at one point and two other dudes that were asking about it are all dead. Get the fuck outta here."

I threw my hands up. "So you want me to believe that some rich old white dude and his privileged daughter hired somebody to take out three guys over a comic book cover. A cover, mind you, that probably isn't worth all that much money, at least not to them. Chandler's probably got the money that thing is worth in his front pocket right now. C'mon, Donnie, what sense does that make?"

Donnie stopped moving stuff and looked at me. "It doesn't make sense to US, yeah. But I bet it makes sense to them. They know something about it that we don't. And three people got killed over it. I'm TELLING you, Farrar, this shit is all on them."

I sighed and rolled my eyes. If Donnie believed this then there was nothing I could do about it. I just had to do as much damage control as I could.

"Ok," I said. "You want to think that, I can't stop you. But don't do anything stupid." Now I sounded like Tidyman. Look how that turned out. "Three dudes are dead and if you think they're dead because of this then don't get yourself fucked up because you're pissed."

Donnie didn't say anything and sat back down at his computer. He stared at it and moved the mouse around but I don't think he was really doing anything.

"You hear me?"

Donnie waved a hand at me and said "Yeah, ok. I hear you. Nothing stupid. Now get the fuck out of here, Farrar."

"You know what?" I said, crossing the room over to Donnie faster than I thought I was capable of. A look of fear came over his face and he almost fell out of the chair again trying to back away. He tried to get up but I held him down with my left hand and stuck a finger into his chest.

"Don't try to flex on me, you fat fuck," I said. "You set me up to have your cousin and his stupid friend lean on me. I didn't forget that. If he didn't end up dead I would still be beating the shit out of you. Don't ever do some shit like that to me again. Ever. Or I will put you in the hospital for an extended fuckin' stay. Do you understand me?"

"Yes." said Donnie in a small voice. I had never seen him like this. Maybe I needed him to screw me over and have me threaten his life more often. I turned from him and went for the door but couldn't really leave like this.

"Listen, " I said, not even looking back at him. "I know Tommy getting killed is eating at you. Now I really don't think it had anything to do with this. I really don't. Just try to stay cool and don't go accusing people of shit that you THINK they did. Let the cops figure it out. If I find out anything about the cover or anything I'll let you know. Why, I don't know. But I will. Ok?"

It was quiet for a second and then Donnie murmured "Ok." That was enough for me. I think my point, especially my initial one, had been made.

I went through the office door, left it open and headed through the store and towards the entrance. Everybody who had been in there when I first showed up was still there and watched me go. I saw one of the *Magic: The Gathering* kids crane his neck to look into Donnie's office, like maybe I had killed him or something. Adventure Time kid was back behind the register but was still giving me seriously hard looks. As my dad used to say, he was a little light in the ass to be looking at people like that but I let it go. Like I said, the kid kinda weirded me out.

I went out to the Jeep and was doing a quick walkaround to make sure my tires weren't slashed when I felt my phone buzz. It was a text that read:

Hi Will, it's Michael Rothstein. Well, forget about it being that Action Comics 309 cover. Found out some guy in Indiana owns it. Oh well, there goes my Kennedy theory. But I still wanna know what the deal is! Text me when you find it, ok?

I texted back *Thx, will do* and leaned against the Jeep to think. I had to call Jessica and tell her that my newest buddies were now in the morgue and then resume the search for this damn cover. I was trying to figure out how exactly I should go about that when I noticed that Adventure Time was staring at me through the store window, hate in his little beady eyes.

I'd had enough Williamsburg for one day so I got in my Jeep and drove away.

10

"They're dead?" said Jessica Chandler.

I was on the phone sitting in front of my apartment building in the Jeep with the windows rolled down. A nice breeze was blowing through the car and I wanted to savor it. The winter had been cold with tons of snow so I would enjoy any pleasant spring day that came along. It would be 90 degrees with 90 percent humidity before I knew it.

"Yeah. Shot to death."

"What? Oh my God. How do you know this?"

I told her about going to see the cops and how the main dude was Donnie's cousin.

"That sonuvabitch. His cousin? He set you up. That bastard."

"Yeah, that's pretty much how I felt."

"But who killed them?" said Jessica and then she gasped. "They don't think you did, do they?"

"They said they didn't. I don't think they do. I don't think they believe these guys getting blasted has anything to do with the fight we had or the Superman cover."

"Well, that's good. I mean, how could it? It's just some comic art."

"That's what I thought. That would seem a little extreme."

She laughed. "Yeah, I think it's a little much, too. Just as long as they don't suspect you. You didn't tell them you gave me the number, did you? I don't want to talk to the cops."

"No, I kept that to myself. Didn't seem necessary."

"Thank you. I called our friend with the police and left a message but he hasn't even gotten back to us yet. Guess I'll just tell him to forget it. So now what? I mean, about finding the art."

I leaned further back in the seat and watched a jet high above the apartment rooftops heading westward. Most likely leaving from JFK or LaGuardia. Heading where? Chicago? Vegas? Los Angeles? I'd take any of those right now. Any chance to be away and to forget my goofy problems and enjoy myself, really enjoy myself. I'd forgotten what that was like.

"Will?" said Jessica.

"Sorry. My mind was drifting there. Not sure. I just have to keep plugging away and asking questions. That art is out there somewhere and I just have to stumble across the person who has it. It just hasn't happened yet."

"Ok. Well, keep me posted. I'm dying to tell dad you found it, for lack of a better term. And if anything else comes up with those two guys getting killed, let me know. As you can imagine, I'm not going to tell dad about that."

I laughed. "Yeah, kinda figured. Ok. Be in touch."

I hung up before I said something stupid and then sat there and thought for a bit. I didn't know what else to do about finding this art, I just found out three people I knew were dead and I was hungry and hadn't eaten all day. There was only one of those that I could do anything about at the moment so I got out of the Jeep, locked it up and headed inside.

Pierre was at the front desk so I let him bust my chops about Jessica and Karen for a few minutes. He was getting a kick out of it so I just laughed along with him. Sometimes you just gotta take your lumps in life.

When I got upstairs and opened the door Thor was just coming out of the kitchen. A water or chow break apparently. A break from exactly what I don't know. Sleeping or slapping balled up papers around, I guess.

Taxing.

"Hey," I said. Thor stopped and gave me a "Hurry it up, I've got some important dozing to get back to" look of semi interest.

"The cops called me cause those two guys I got into it with yesterday are dead. Yep, dead. Shot. Isn't that crazy?"

Thor looked at me for a few seconds and then turned and slowly sauntered back into the bedroom.

"I know, right?" I said. "I thought it was a big deal, too." But of course, Thor didn't come back or meow or anything like that because sarcasm is lost on cats. I really must remember that.

I went into the kitchen and opened the fridge not really expecting to find anything I wanted. What I really wanted was a burger. A good ol' double with cheddar cheese and onions and mushrooms and maybe some avocado. Oh, yeah, some avocado. That sounded good. And some fries, those big fat steak fries, not the skinny ones. I definitely wasn't gonna find that in this fridge. Not unless two bottles of Pepsi, 3 slices of Kraft American cheese, leftover Chinese food, some chicken wings and a jar of spaghetti sauce could somehow be magically combined to create one. Not even Doctor Strange could do that. Damn. Where could I get a good burger like that? Downtown Brooklyn? I was trying to think of burger places downtown to go to when my phone rang and I saw it was Coleman Chandler's line. Oh, great. Another status report that will be exactly like the last status report. But when I answered I was surprised to hear Coleman Chandler's voice.

"Mr. Farrar, I just received a disturbing phone call from our mutual friend Donnie Castiglia. Very disturbing, actually. What's all this about his cousin?"

Goddammit, Donnie. "I'm sorry, I didn't want him to bother you with this. I told him this didn't have anything to do with you but...well, I guess he felt the need to call you."

"He made some very severe accusations against me and my daughter. We need to discuss this."

I put my head in my hand and sighed. I couldn't believe Donnie went there but why couldn't I? Clearly stupid Donnie was capable of anything, even after telling he wouldn't do it. I wanted to drive back over to his place and throw him down a flight of stairs. No, two flights of stairs. It may cause some structural damage to whatever building we were in and maybe a slight tremor but I would risk it. Stupid, stupid bastard.

"I'm really sorry, Mr. Chandler," I said. "See, the other day I was-"

"Mr. Farrar, at this advanced stage of my life, having a long conversation on the phone ranks right up there with getting a colonoscopy and "loaning" my daughter a tremendous sum of money to bail her out of whatever crisis she has put herself into. In other words, I hate speaking on the phone. Where are you now?"

"Um… at home. I just walked in."

"Well, I apologize for this but could you possibly come out and see me to talk about this? Would that be possible?"

Oh, well. I guess I could eat on the run. Or after I spoke to Chandler. Or I could just starve to death and be done with this whole business. That actually sounded preferable.

"Sure," I said, trying to mask my reluctance. "I'll leave in a few minutes." I looked at my watch. It was a little after three o'clock. Damn, a lot had gone on since I got on the train to head to Midtown. What a day.

"Fine. Jessica won't be here when you arrive but Rick will be. He'll let you in."

Oh, joy. Maybe the two us could have a knife fight or something. That would cap my day off perfectly.

I said ok, hung up and looked up the Verrazano Bridge way of getting to South Orange. It was a ten buck plus trip that way because of the toll but I didn't want to go through the city at that time. Besides, I needed something different. Although the last few days were about as different as I could want.

After heading down and taking some more joking from Pierre I was on my way to the Prospect Expressway and the

Gowanus which fed into the big bridge. It seemed a goofy way to go, basically backwards to go forwards, but Google Maps always gives you the least complicated so I didn't fight it. It was probably faster than crawling through the Brooklyn streets to get there, making a million stops at lights.

I guess I had turned my radio off earlier when heading to see the cops because I suddenly became aware that no one was yelling about sports. After turning on ESPN radio I found out the Mets were on. Completely forgot they had a day game. When I tuned in the Mets were batting, up one to nothing in the 7th with Howie Rose and Josh Lewin on the call, as usual. Excellent. I leaned back in the seat and just tried to enjoy the ride. Baseball always has a way of making me comfortable. I've heard people call baseball boring and I've never understood that. The pace was just right when you needed a break from searching for comic book pages and dealing with people getting shot to death.

Eventually I made it to the Verrazano and then crossed onto Staten Island. I have actually never set foot in Staten Island, despite all the times I've been through it. And I don't count taking the ferry and then going from one dock to another to take the next one back to Manhattan. I've never had any reason to go. Besides possibly the Wu-Tang Clan, I don't know anyone from the rugged lands of Shaolin as they called it. But the way this search was going I could see me actually having to actually walk around here. Maybe I should drive back home through the Bronx just to complete this whole five borough tour of New York thing I was doing.

Traffic was light so soon I was through the island and onto the Goethals Bridge, which connects Shaolin to New Jersey. When I was a kid I used to think that it was the Gotham Bridge and that we were heading to Gotham City with the possibility of seeing Batman or getting murdered by the Joker. Preferably seeing Batman.

The Mets managed to squeak out a win though they tried their best to give me a heart attack, as usual. They got out of a bases loaded one out jam to nail down a 3-2 win just as I was getting on the turnpike. And by the time the post game show was over I was off of I-78 and driving through Union, New Jersey only a few towns over from South Orange. Only then did I give in and start to think about what stupid Donnie might've said to Chandler. I wanted to pull over, call him up and scream at him but I needed to hear it from Chandler first. I had no idea what Donnie said, though I could imagine. If it was anything like he told me earlier, and judging from what Chandler said it sounded like it was, then this was getting real ugly real fast.

Soon I was pulling up to the gate at the Chandler residence and punching the call box button. It was silent for about thirty seconds and then the gate staring moving slowly open. Yep, my buddy Rick was here all right. I drove up to the garage area and parked, not at all looking forward to dealing with him and Chandler.

By the time I got to the front door it was open and my pal was waiting for me. He had on another tight black t-shirt but no shorts today. Instead he was wearing a pair of black, white and gray striped Zubaz. Stylish. I started to walk by but he cleared his throat and when I looked at him he just stared at the floor, obviously uneasy. What was this?

"Listen, um…" Rick shifted his weight from foot to foot nervously and put his hands in his pockets. "We got off to a bad start the other day. I know you're trying to find this cover and… well… after that fat jackass was here I didn't trust anyone to do the right thing by Mr. Chandler. I know you're really trying to find it. I screwed up and let it get taken in the first place. So… I appreciate it."

Poor Rick. He looked like he would rather have been run over by the Bentley than have to say that to me. I have to admit, his whole body language made me want to laugh but there was no point in being an ass about it so I offered my hand. He took it, begrudgingly.

"No problem. I understand. And I really do want to find that art. So anything you can remember or think of, please let me know."

Rick nodded and we stood there for a second not saying anything. Awkward.

"Chandler's, uh.... in the sunroom. Do you need me to take you?"

I shook my head no and then we stood some seconds more before Rick said "Ok." and walked outside, closing the door behind him. He probably needed to go behind some shrubs to throw up. That whole scene was tougher than calculus for him.

I made all the twists and turns and through the kitchen and stared out at the gazebo again before I slowly made my way to the sunroom door. I really didn't feel like having this conversation. I didn't know exactly what the conversation would be but I knew I wasn't going to be overjoyed about it. Might as well get it over with. I paused for a second outside and then went in.

He looked exactly as he looked when I saw him two days before. If we hadn't gone upstairs that day I would've thought he was in here the whole time. He sat in the same chair, with the same looking drink and what appeared to be the exact same clothes on. They probably weren't. That last shirt's color was probably called Bleached Bone and this one was probably called Brilliant Cloud or something stupid like that. Or maybe he was like Einstein and had a closet full of the same exact ensemble. But Einstein was a genius. If you or

I did that we would be called crazy.

Chandler motioned to me from his chair. "Come in, Mr. Farrar."

I took the seat I had last time and settled in. The sunroom looked exactly the same the same as well except that maybe the sky was a little cloudier. I thought I had heard that some rain was coming. But other than that it was pretty much like before.

"Would you like something to drink?" asked Chandler, lifting his mystery beverage.

"No. Thank you."

"Alight," He took a sip. "Now, Mr. Farrar, would you kindly explain to me why Mr. Castiglia would accuse my daughter and me of murder?"

I said "Ahhhh, boy....," put my face in my hands and leaned forward in my seat. Donnie, Donnie, Donnie.... there was really nothing left to say or do but to kill him. I mean, what else was there?

"It's.... kind of a convoluted story, Mr. Chandler."

"I'm a relatively intelligent person, Mr. Farrar. I'm sure I can follow along. Start from the beginning."

So I did. I told him about all the different people who seem to be looking for the page, about the fight with the two Guidos, their deaths, Poon being dead and me beating up Donnie. I pretty much told him everything. Again, I left out the whole sex with his daughter part. That might've just been too much. But I told him that Jessica and I had spoken about the murders.

"Jessica didn't tell me any of this," said Chandler. "Even after Donnie called. She claimed she didn't know anything about what was going on."

Nice backing me up, Jess. I thought.

"Are we certain that these two gentleman getting killed has anything to do with my missing art?" said Chandler.

"No, not at all. The police implied that they were troublemakers. Anybody could've smoked them."

"And this fellow, Ken Tang. Do we even know if somebody killed him?"

"No, sir."

"Then I don't understand what Castiglia is talking about."

"Yeah, he's really leaping to conclusions. I really think he's just got it in for you since you fired him. And he definitely tried to get that page to hold it over your head."

Chandler shook his head. "Mr. Castiglia also says that he knows where the art is. He said he could have by the days end."

I laughed. "No, he can't. He has no idea where it is. If he knew he would have it and would be trying to wring more money out of you."

"Why would he say that?"

"Who knows? It's just another dopey ploy to somehow squeeze you. Don't pay any attention to him."

Chandler sighed and stroked his bony chin. "This has become way more complicated than I thought possible. Do you think you can find this page, Mr. Farrar? Without this further becoming a circus?"

To be honest, I really wasn't sure. Poon was gone and he was the last person to have it. I couldn't just keep bugging his mother about it, either. Her son was dead and she probably didn't know anything about it. For all I knew, Poon sold the page to somebody else who was outside of all the comic art dealing circles. I didn't have a whole lot of leads. All I had was a bunch of people trying to find the same thing that I was. Well, minus two people anyway. But there were still mysteries with this, some unknown participants. Michael Rothstein had said that another person had called him on the page. Who was that? And although I didn't trust Rick I didn't want to stat throwing his name into it with Chandler. He probably wouldn't react well.

But with all that I still wanted to find that art badly. I had gotten my teeth into this problem and I wanted to see it through.

"Yes," I said. "Give me time but yes, I will find it. After all this nonsense, I really do want to."

Chandler stared at me for a moment and then said, "Yes, I really do believe you do."

We sat quietly for a few seconds and I could hear the muted sounds of lawnmowers in the distance. Probably right next door for all I knew. The sunroom seemed like it really kept sound out. Thank goodness with all the yard work going on around here. What, they do it everyday?

"Well, I greatly appreciate you coming out here and giving me an update," said Chandler. "And I also greatly appreciate you trying to protect me from the... extracurricular business associated with this."

"No problem, sir," I said, rising. "You shouldn't have to deal with that. All you should have to deal with is getting that art in your hands. The rest is my job."

He offered his hand, still seated. Another exhausting day of going up and down the stairs, I guess. I shook it and then turned to leave. I was fully trusted to show myself out again.

"Thank you," said Chandler behind me. I turned back from the doorway and for some reason at that moment he seemed even older than before. A cloud passed in front of the sun and the room got gray and shadowed. Chandler seemed so small in that chair and in that big, dark glass room surrounded by all of his giant plants and flowers. You could lose him in there. Maybe that was why he liked it so much.

"No problem," I said again and wove my way through the house and out.

11

Rick was nowhere to be found when I got outside. Probably somewhere doing squat thrusts. Or putting away his listening devices. Or both. Maybe he was a multi-tasker.

The big, dark cloud had passed and it was back to being sunny but it seemed cooler to me. A breeze rustled the roses and tulips that bordered the driveway and parking area and the trees above swayed slightly, the leaves shushing in the wind. I remembered that it was supposed to rain either tonight or tomorrow and vowed to do all my future investigating in the comfort of my own home. Screw all this legwork stuff.

I also vowed to finally eat something. It was 4:37 and a revolt was going on inside my stomach. I still had the taste for burger but I didn't want to go to Stony's again. I sat in the Jeep and Googled burger places in North Jersey until I noticed that there was a Smashburger on Route 10, not really that far from where I was. I hadn't had a Smashburger in at least two months. Sold. I put the Jeep in drive and headed over to Northfield Avenue, which basically runs right into Route 10. Then I put on *Star Time,* the four disc box set of James Brown. *The Funky Drummer* never failed to cheer me up.

On my way over I considered my options and I came to the extraordinary conclusion that I really didn't have any. I had to hope that I would stumble across something or hear from somebody that caught wind of the art's whereabouts. That wasn't really a plan but unless I could think of another course of action, that was all I had.

By the time I had gotten to Smashburger I had thought of a few more people outside of New York who I could get in touch with, two of who were in California and one in Florida. Maybe they heard something, some chatter that no one hear was hearing. Anything was possible. When I got home I would get in touch.

I wheeled into the lot and was just about to get out of the car when my phone rang. When I saw who it was, I was stunned. No way. There was no way.

I pressed the phone screen and said, "Donnie, you have got to have the biggest balls in the world to be calling me right now. Got to."

"Listen," said Donnie.

"You're kidding, right? You can't seriously expect me to have a conversation with you."

He laughed and I wanted to blow up all of Williamsburg just to make sure I got him.

"You're still mad about that? I'm the one that should be mad. My cousin is dead."

"No, you stupid fuck. You called up Chandler and accused him and his daughter of murder. That's the new thing that I'm mad at you about."

Donnie sucked his teeth and said, "Oh yeah, that. You know, I wish I could've seen that old man's face when I dropped that shit on him."

I hit the end button and got out of the car. By the time I had crossed the parking lot and gotten to the door he was calling again.

"What the hell is wrong with you?" I said after I answered. "I mean, really. What is wrong with you?"

"Farrar, listen to me. Don't hang up. Just listen. Ok?"

I looked up into the sky and wondered why I was even entertaining this. I moved away from the front of Smashburger and started heading back to my car.

"What?" I said, climbing in. "And make fuckin' sense or I will hang up again."

"Ok. Ok. You and I really need to sit down and put our heads together about this situation."

"Donnie, the only thing I want to put your head together with is a brick wall."

Donnie chuckled. "That's funny. Seriously. I have a plan and I need your help with it."

"A plan. What the hell are you talking about, Donnie? I told you to make sense. You told Chandler that you know where the art is? You're full of shit, Donnie. What the hell are you doing?""

"Just stirring up some shit. To see what would happen."

"And something happened?"

There was a pause on the other end, like he was trying to decide if he should tell me something. I watched a man take a small boy and slightly older girl, presumably his kids, into SmashBurger. They all looked pretty happy, like they had been looking forward to it. My stomach growled and it sounded like a mountain lion was living in me. When in the world would I finally get to eat?

"Nothing specific happened," Donnie finally said. "That's why I need to talk with you."

"You are talking with me. Now what do you want?"

"No, no. I need you to come out to the store. Tonight."

I almost dropped my phone. "What? Are you crazy? I'm not coming over to you tonight. No, fuck that. You talk to me now and tell me what's up. What kind of shit are you trying to pull?"

"Farrar, no, no," Donnie said. He sounded almost desperate. "I need you to come here. I can't talk now, I gotta leave in a few minutes, I gotta see my aunt and uncle... funeral plans, family shit... it's a fuckin' mess. I won't be able to talk until later."

"So call me later. Why do I have to drag my ass over to you?"

"Because I don't want to talk about this over the phone, Farrar. I got theories and ideas and they're gonna sound crazy over the phone."

"And they're gonna make sense in person? No."

"I'll give you fifty dollars. All you have to do is come over here at ten tonight and I'll give you fifty dollars."

I almost dropped the phone again. Donnie was one of the cheapest people I had ever known. For him to offer up fifty bucks was insane. He must have been really desperate. I thought about it for a second and then decided to take advantage of it.

"One hundred dollars," I said. "One hundred and you Paypal it to me right now. That's the only way."

"A hundred dollars? Fuck, Farrar...'

"Right now or forget it. You've caused me all kinds of trouble over the last few days. I don't have any more time for your bullshit."

There was a long pause and some cursing and grumbling that I couldn't make out and then he said "Alright, dammit. Give me your email again." I did and he told me to hang on. I guess he put his phone down because there was a lot of rustling and then I could hear him in the background tapping on a keyboard and getting annoyed.

"You can call me back, you know?" I said loudly but he couldn't hear me over his angry typing and mumbling. I drummed my fingers on the steering wheel and briefly considered turning James Brown back on but it would probably be only a few minutes before Donnie came back and continued making my day into a nightmare. So I just sat back and checked out the parking lot. Smashburger is in a little strip mall so there were a lot of people heading to the other stores and cars coming off of Route 10 and into the lot. But it seemed like a good amount of people were heading to get food. It was early for dinner but maybe everybody had their lunch ruined too and had to wait until now to eat. At least I wasn't the only sucker. Then I saw two brothas walking out of Smashburger looking all happy and full. One of them had the nerve to be rubbing his stomach. Lucky bastards.

The Paypal app on my phone chimed and I saw that I had one hundred dollars sent to me. Son of a bitch. I thought for sure Donnie would come up with some nonsense to get out of paying me. I sent it to my bank account and then got back on the phone.

"I got it."

"Ok, great," said Donnie, annoyed. "NOW will you be over here tonight at ten or what?"

"Yes, I'll be there. Jeez."

"Great. Come in the back way. There's an alley that runs behind the store. My office door opens to that. You'll see the sign, just knock."

"Ok. But if I find that you're just wasting my time I'm out."

"Oh, no. This will not be a waste of your time. I think you'll find it very interesting."

"Wait, " I said. "You're sounding all mysterious and shit. What's going on? What did you do?"

"I told you what I did. I stirred up some trouble, I made some noise. Threw shit out there. We'll see if something comes of it."

I had no idea what he was talking about but I just went along with him and said, "So was accusing Chandler of murder part of stirring up trouble? An old man who just wants a piece of comic art that his dead buddy left him?"

Donnie laughed. "Well, man, you know what they say. You can't break an omelet without making a few eggs." He paused for a moment and then said, "Wait. That ain't right, is it?"

"No," I said. "No, it is not."

"Well, fuck it. You knew what I meant. I stirred shit up and now I'm gonna get me some answers." Then he must've felt really sure about himself because he tried it again. "Like they say, you can't make an egg with breaking a few… ah, shit."

"Have fun with that," I said and hung up.

12

I took my sweet time eating my double cheeseburger with fries and drinking my strawberry shake and watching all the people come and go through the strip mall. I knew that if I drove home right now, there was no way I was coming back out to go to Williamsburg. A hundred dollars be damned. I would kick my sneakers off and open a Pepsi and Thor would jump on my lap and it would be a wrap. Game over. So I leisurely downed my meal, though I was completely starving and then sat there, thinking about how to waste more time. It was 6:11 and I was truly in no hurry. I had almost four hours to kill.

I remembered the comic book store in Livingston I had

visited the other day and decided to get over there before closing time. It seemed like three months ago when I ran into Eddie at Midtown Comics and he gave me the bad news about Poon. It was the same damn day. I swore again to not leave the apartment at all the next day and went out to the Jeep.

I cruised up Route 10 and then around the traffic circle to where Route 10 became Mt. Pleasant Avenue and then up the hill through Livingston. Traffic was cooperating although I didn't need it to and I got to New World Manga in fifteen minutes. It was completely dark by the time I parked and getting cooler by the minute. The wind had picked up a bit felt more like a late fall day than an early spring one. Which I guess can kind of feel the same, when you think about it. Stupid fat Donnie. I didn't want to be out later. I wanted to be drinking soda and shooting people in the warmth and comfort of my own home.

Luckily for me, New World Manga stayed open until eight o'clock and I milked that for all it was worth. But by 8:03 I was back in the Jeep with three trade paperbacks, a Godzilla figure and an issue of *The Amazing World of Gumball*. I didn't know how the comic would be but that I love that cartoon. Ah, Gumball Watterson, you little scamp.

Now that is was after eight, I could seriously start to think about getting to Brooklyn. I decided to take the 280 way back to the city since I was right near the highway anyway. 280 always got bogged down at Newark where the William A. Stickel Memorial Bridge crossed the Passaic River and connected Newark with Harrison. I have no idea who William A. Stickel was but I remembered reading the name of the bridge once and never forgetting it for some reason. Well, the Willie A. was a nightmare at rush hour and beyond, normally. I could definitely count on some time being chewed up there. Or so I thought. You could imagine my surprise when the bridge was free and clear along with the rest of 280. It was smooth sailing all the way to Jersey City and the Holland Tunnel.

In fact, everything was just way too cooperative. Even Canal Street had minimal traffic. What the hell? I briefly considered stopping in Manhattan but convinced myself that the BQE would be a mess. I was, sadly, wrong. The next thing I knew I was in Williamsburg. Again.

I found a spot on Penn Street four blocks from Blastaar and looked at the dash clock. 8:52. Wow, I was REALLY early. After sitting there for a few minutes listening to sports radio I said screw it and turned off the ignition. I wasn't gonna sit and twiddle my thumbs for over an hour just to fit Donnie's fat ass schedule. I started to get out but a cool blast of air came in when I opened the door and I closed it quickly. Yikes, it had gotten chilly out there. There was a black Nike hoodie on the backseat and I put that on, thanking myself for keeping it in the Jeep. Then I got out, locked up and started walking.

The streets were very quiet and very dark. Maybe it wasn't any darker than usual but it sure seemed like it. The streetlights were a dim looking orange that barely seemed to illuminate the building fronts and cars. There wasn't too much foot traffic out, just a few people who looked like they just wanted to get from point A to point B as quickly as possible. I didn't blame them. Even with the hoodie on I was cold. I quickly walked down Penn, turned right on Lee Avenue and then turned right again on Hooper Street. Another gust of cold air rudely met me at the corner and I quickened my pace, vainly trying to zip the hoodie up even more. About fifty feet up the street was the alley entrance Donnie mentioned and I rushed over to it, coming to an abrupt stop at the entrance. It's always a good plan to check out an alley before you just go charging in, at least in my experience. You might have a bum doing something not right or a wild dog or who-the-hell-knows-what going in there. But this alley was fairly clean, well lit and, most importantly, empty.

It was much wider than I thought it would be. It actually served as a service and delivery entrance for the stores on Lee Avenue and was big enough for a decent sized delivery truck to pull into comfortably. I could've parked the Jeep here and saved myself a little walk. I briefly considered going back to get it but what for? Now or later I'd still walking. Might as well do it later and keep going.

The sign over the Blastaar rear entrance was smaller and less crazy than the one out front. It was just a simple printed white sign with the address over a narrow beige door, lit by a single dim bulb mounted in the brick above it. I walked up to the door and was just about to knock when I noticed that it was slightly open. Maybe Donnie had left it like that for me? I listened for a second, heard nothing and then rapped on the peeling wood. Still nothing. I leaned closer to the narrow opening and said "Donnie?", trying to be loud enough but quiet enough at the same time. More nothing. I stood there in the dim light and the cold and thought about it. I've seen enough movies and TV shows to know that this could be the start of a very bad scene. Maybe I'd seen too many movies and TV shows and was just overreacting. Maybe Donnie was in the bathroom and this was nowhere near as creepy as it appeared. Maybe. But if he tried to pull some crazy shit I was gonna take him out. No questions. I took a deep breath, pushed the door open with my knuckles and slowly stepped in.

The room was a complete shambles. A small lamp sat leaning against the wall in the farthest corner, the only source of light. Papers and boxes littered the floor. Anything that had been closed was now ripped open, it's contents rifled through. What the hell happened here? I went back to the door, pushed it close with my foot and slowly moved back into the room, taking everything in. All the filing cabinets had been left open, whatever papers that were inside gone through and thrown around. The desk that Donnie was at the day before had been searched, all of its drawers opened and the blotter riffled through and thrown aside. The computer had been upended and the keyboard leaned against it, long way up. All the junk I had seen on the desk was now on the floor, scattered everywhere. The big black office chair lay on its back next to the desk and next to the chair laid Donnie.

He was naked except for white boxer shorts and white tube socks, one with a huge hole in the front that three of his toes stuck through. Donnie lay on his side with his arms pulled over his head, his hands tied with an electrical cord that was secured at the other end to one of the desk legs. There was a gag in his mouth, a handkerchief that was tied around his head. He was looking right at me, his eyes wide and with a look of fear that I had never seen on a person before. But I didn't have to get closer to know that he wasn't seeing anything. Blastaar was done seeing forever.

I had seen a few dead bodies before. A shooting, a car

accident, a fall from a roof. But I had never seen anything like this. It was beyond cruel and seeing him like that with his eyes wide open… I felt a little sick and had to turn away. How could someone do this? Why? I got myself under control mentally and physically and steeled myself to look again.

I crept closer. Half smoked cigarettes lay all around Donnie's huge body, some just barely. There were matches too, at least a dozen of them, all struck and burned to a shrivel. Scorch marks dotted the linoleum floor under most of them. Had somebody knocked over an ashtray? But I looked closer at Donnie. On his body, even visible through the thick black body hair were small dark burns. His chest and stomach were covered with them.

Somebody had tortured Donnie to death.

I went around his body and stood listening at the door that led inside to the store. It was quiet in there, too. I checked the door but it was locked on my side. I stood perfectly still and tried to take in all the sounds I could but there was just the occasional car going by the front of the store and nothing else. Silence.

I still didn't understand what had happened here. It didn't seem like any kind of real robbery. What were they searching for? Donnie had said he started some shit. Had he tried to lure whoever killed his cousin here? Was this actually because of the Superman cover?

I braced my back against the door leading to the store and tried to talk myself out of believing that. But Poon was dead, two guys trying to strong-arm me for the art were dead and now Donnie was a goner and his office a wreck. I had to seriously start thinking it was all connected. Donnie probably floated the notion that he had the art, just opened up his big stupid mouth and put it out there. To who? And he probably wanted me here as backup so we can apprehend the bad guys like we were the fucking Hardy Boys. But apparently the killers showed up early and threw a wrench into those little plans. Nice, Donnie. You probably would've gotten me killed too.

So here I was, alone with a dead man, a man I had punched earlier and had arranged to meet late it night solo. Goddammit. I took a quick look around for Donnie's phone. All of our communications were on there, any record of us having talked. I knelt down, looked under the desk and in the trash. Nothing. It really didn't matter, the cops would find everything out. They would know. Tidyman was gonna absolutely love this shit.

I was considering whether or not to call the cops, to go all pre-emptive and try and ride it out that way when I glanced at a digital clock that was sitting crookedly on a stack of new *Batman* comics. It was only 9:28. That's right, I was early. If I could get back to the city fast enough....

I took another look around and then quickly went to the exit door. I was pretty sure I hadn't touched anything with my fingers. I didn't think I did. Now, I was doubting myself. But I didn't want to rub down anything and wipe away something useful for the cops. As it was I would have to use my shirt to turn the doorknob. Damn.

I opened the door slowly, peeked out and stepped into the alley. I took another look inside making sure I didn't leave anything behind and one more at Donnie. He still laid there, his hands bound, his mouth gagged and that awful look of terror in his eyes. I wish I could've untied him and covered him. I felt terrible leaving him like that. But I couldn't. The cops had to see this.

My dad used to say that dying never made anybody a better person. That was definitely the case with Donnie. But he didn't deserve to be tied up and tortured with lit cigarettes until he died. He was never that bad a human being.

You can't break an omelet without making a few eggs.

I took one last look, whispered "Sorry, Donnie." and closed the door.

13

"So let me see if I understand this," said Detective Tidyman, his hands clasped behind his head. He leaned far back in his battered chair and it let out a long agonizing screech that sounded like a strangled duck but he didn't seem to notice. "Three days ago, Tommy Castiglia and his boy turn up dead. Double tapped in his car. Then just two days later somebody makes an ashtray outta his cousin Donnie and he checks out, too. All of these knuckleheads are connected, in the past few days, to you... and yet you know nothing about this. How does that work?"

I was sitting in the 110th again, in the same dirty hard chair facing the same dirty desk with the same two cops staring at me. At least Himes was dressed differently this time, sporting a charcoal gray suit and dark red tie. Tidyman looked exactly the same as far as I could tell. And manacled guy was gone. Probably sleeping in lockup somewhere.

I stared past Tidyman and out the window towards the airport. There was no chance of seeing a jet now as it had started raining late the night before and had gotten consistently heavier all through the morning, visibility made practically nil by the clouds and constant downpour. It was a gray and cold and generally miserable day, which seemed to fit. At least I could see the sky. If I were in an interrogation room I would be in deep shit.

"I don't know how it works." I said. "I just know that it does. I don't what the hell is going on."

Tidyman stared at me few a few seconds and then sighed. "Give it to me again."

I sighed, too, dramatically. I was nervous now, worried I would slip up. Just say what you said before, I told myself. Keep it simple.

I lucked out the night before, or at least I hoped I had. I made it back to the Jeep as fast as I could without running, started her up and got on the BQE heading north towards Queens. Traffic was still light and I was on the 59th Street Bridge then over Roosevelt Island and into Midtown Manhattan really quickly. I hadn't dared to look at the time until I was in the city but I did then and was relieved it was only 10:02. I must've set a land speed record getting to Manhattan. Then I shot across town to the west side and only then, when I was on 7th Avenue and 52nd, did I pull over and use my cell. I made two calls about two minutes apart, both of which I knew wouldn't be answered and left a message after the second one. Then I found a McDonalds on Broadway between 51st and 52nd, went in and bought a Double Quarter Pounder with Cheese, making sure I put the receipt in my wallet. After that I sat in the Jeep, watched theater goers and others hustle too and fro in the cold night and tried to come to grips with what I saw. Then I drove home. And now I would see if my little skullduggery would pay off.

I had gotten the call a lot earlier than I expected. I guess one of the guys who worked at Blastaar's had shown up early and found Donnie. It wouldn't have taken long for it to get to Tidyman and Himes, who were looking into Donnie's cousin's death already. So at 8:03 a.m. after a fitful and strange night of attempted sleep, I got another call inviting me down to the station. I guess it was better than them coming to get me.

"I was supposed to see Donnie last night at ten," I said. "But I screwed around in the city and I ended up late. Honestly I didn't want to go over there. I was tired. I called him to say I wouldn't see him until tomorrow. Being today."

"You called twice."

"Yeah. And I left him the message the second time when I didn't get him. I didn't want to go all the way out there and he not be there."

"And you were where when you called?"

"I was in Manhattan for both calls. Somewhere, I don't remember where. Midtown, I guess. I was already late. I figured I would get at him today."

Tidyman nodded and studied a sheet of paper. I had no idea how sophisticated the cops were with cell phone calls now but I was sure they could figure out from the towers where I was when I called. Calling Donnie from the city was my best move. If I had called while I was in the store I'm sure I would've been in cuffs by now.

"And where were you before that? Before you were in Manhattan?"

"I was in Jersey. I was running some errands and then I went to a comic store in Livingston."

Tidyman shook his head. You guys and your comics. Jesus. And then what?"

"And then I drove to the city. I wasn't in any big hurry. I had plenty of time before I had to see Donnie. But I kinda lost track of time."

"Anything else to prove you were in the city at that

time?" said Tidyman, looking up from the paper.

I acted annoyed. "Jesus, I don't know... oh, wait. Wait." I got my wallet out, fumbled through it and pulled out the McDonalds receipt. "I stopped at Mickey D's. I forgot about that."

He took the receipt and studied it. I already knew it said 10:22 P.M. on it. Tidyman smirked. "Convenient."

I gave him a hurt look. "What? I keep all my receipts."

"Nice to be organized." Tidyman blew out some air and then looked at Himes. Giving the new guy a shot at me. Himes leaned forward and said "And you were coming to see him why?"

"I honestly don't know. He insisted that I come out to the store but he wasn't really clear on it. He just said that it had to do with this cover I'm looking for."

"The Superman cover. And what's going on with that?"

"Nothing. I can't find it. I don't have any leads. Donnie made it sound like he had some ideas about finding it but wouldn't say what those were until I came out there. I didn't really believe he had anything."

"So what did you think?"

"I have no idea. But if he didn't have anything solid I wasn't gonna run over there at 10:00 at night. It could wait."

"Well..." said Tidyman, looking sideways out the window. "He had some kinda info. Enough to have somebody play tic tac toe on him."

"But I don't know what. I don't know what this would have to do with that artwork. I really don't. I seriously doubt somebody would do this to him over some comic art."

Himes shook his head. "You said this page was worth maybe ten grand. We've seen people do crazier shit for less."

I couldn't really disagree with that so I just sat there.

"Who are you working for?" asked Tidyman. "Who has you looking for this page?"

"Is that important?"

Tidyman gave me a face. "It is if I'm asking it."

Damn. I had really tried to keep Chandler and Jessica out of this but I had just reached the end of my rope. I sighed and rubbed my face. Had to spill it.

"His name is Coleman Chandler."

A frown crossed Tidyman's face. "Chandler." He picked up the sheet of paper he had earlier and scanned it.

"Donnie placed a call earlier in the day to a C. Chandler." Tidyman put the paper down and looked at me. "Now what was that all about?"

"I have no idea."

"Didn't you say that this Chandler guy fired Donnie 'cause he tried to jack up the price on him?"

"Maybe your boy Chandler had just about enough of him." said Himes.

"Aw, c'mon," I said. "Chandler is, like, a thousand years old."

"So maybe he farmed out the job to a much younger man."

"Who knew Donnie, knew where he worked...." chimed in Tidyman.

"You guys are unbelievable," I said. "Coleman Chandler didn't have Donnie killed and he damn sure didn't ask me to do it. And I was nowhere near his store last night. I didn't even want to be near the guy."

"And I don't suppose you took a little trip over to Sheepshead Bay last night either, right? Maybe on your way home?" said Himes.

I frowned. "No. Why would I go to Sheepshead Bay? That's not on my way home."

"Well, somebody ransacked Donnie's apartment last night. No forced entry. Since we didn't find his keys we assume the killer took 'em and did a little searching."

"Jesus," I said. Donnie must've really convinced whoever these people were that he had the page. And when he croaked as they were trying to get it out of him they went to his place. Boy, they wanted it bad. I just couldn't understand why.

"Now, what time did you get home last night?" asked Tidyman.

"Um... I guess about 11:00," I said. "A little before actually because the doorman was still there."

"He saw you?"

"Yeah, we spoke for a bit. Mets stuff. We always talk Mets stuff. Then I went upstairs."

"Alright," said Tidyman. "So Donnie tells you to come over. Won't really say why. You drive from Jersey to Manhattan and it gets late and you blow him off and go home. And now he's dead."

I shrugged. "I guess, yeah."

"Now, why did he send you a hundred bucks earlier?"

I knew they were going to dig that up so I wasn't surprised. "Because that was the only way I was gonna go over there to see his stupid ass after the shit he pulled. I told him there was no way. But he offered me the money and actually sent it."

Tidyman frowned. "Unusually generous for him, from what I understand."

"Yeah, I thought so too. Maybe he was trying to set me up for something again."

Himes laughed. "You mean like his own murder? Well, he did a damn good job of that, then."

I slumped in my chair and facepalmed myself. Even in death Donnie managed to screw me.

Tidyman took off his glasses and rubbed his tired, worn

face. He put them back on and stared straight up at the ceiling, stretching his arms. "Farrar, I do not like this. You looked like you wanted to seriously fuck Donnie up the other day and here we are with him in the morgue after you had beef with him. Look at it from our perspective."

My phone started vibrating in my pocket. It stopped and started again and I knew it was a call but I didn't feel entirely comfortable answering it. "Excuse me Tidyman, I know you're trying to tie me to three murders and all but I really need to take this." I let it go and eventually it stopped.

"I can only look at it from my mine." I said. "The "I went home and didn't go see him and found out the next day that he was dead and I had nothing whatsoever to do with it" perspective."

Tidyman nodded and just looked at me. He was still leaning back, his head canted to the side. He looked at Himes, who was drumming his fingers on the desk and then back at me with a sly smile on his face. "What would you say if I told you that a person matching your description was seen leaving Blastaar Comics?"

"I would say that was early yesterday afternoon when I was last there. Is there something else I should say?"

Tidyman chuckled and looked sidewise at Himes. "Look at him." he said, pointing his chin at me. "All cool and shit. Better than the other day."

"A pro," nodded Himes. "He's a seasoned pro, now."

I sighed again and rubbed my head with both hands. It already felt like I had been here for an eternity. I just wanted to run, get out of there before something blew up in my face. My phone vibrated again. I'd completely forgotten, in the last three minutes of cops badgering me, that it had rang. Someone had left a message. Check it later.

"Well," said Tidyman. "Because you don't listen to me and are dumb, a bunch of witnesses, including a guy who works for Donnie who would like nothing better than to see you gutted and strung up in Times Square, heard you beat the crap out of our vic only hours before he bought it for good."

I knew Adventure Time Kid would jam me up. He probably made it sound like I had brass knuckles and a spiked bat. Little fuck. Then Tidyman got annoyed and leaned across the desk towards me, his caterpillar eyebrows like angry little awnings over his eyes. "I fucking told you not to do something stupid and you go off and do something stupid. How do you think this looks, Farrar?

"Bad." I said, "I swear, though, I swear I didn't kill him. And I don't know who did or why."

Tidyman and Himes just looked at me and we sat in silence again. All around us cops were on the phone or talking or at their computers so there was sound everywhere but the three of us sat there quietly, as if in a different world. This was making me mental. I had to get the hell out of there.

"Listen," I said. "Do I need a lawyer here?"

Tidyman shrugged. "I don't think so. Not yet. Do you think you need one?"

"No."

"Well, good. Let's not get the lawyers involved then."

They both continued to stare at me, unmoving. It was like looking at an Alex Ross painting. Then a thought popped into my head. Why wasn't I in the interrogation room? They were pretty much doing that now. Unless there was some serious room for doubt, some other leads that needed to be followed up on. Like with Donnie's cousin.

"Hold on," I said. "You guys have access to Donnie's phone records. Did he get a mystery phone call? Like his cousin did? Somebody probably didn't just stroll into his office without him knowing. And he sounded like he had something brewing. Did somebody besides me call him?"

The two detectives continued to look at me like I hadn't even said anything. I slowly sat upright and stared right back.

"Somebody did. And you guys were trying to nail me with this shit. Knowing full well that somebody else called him. Another stolen phone, I bet. Right?"

Tidyman crossed his arms and gave me his hard cop look. "Boy, you sure know an awful lot about a mystery phone call that may or may not have happened, Farrar."

I shook my head and laughed. "Don't even try that on me, Tidyman. There's somebody else running around knocking off people and you know it. And you're trying to hang it around my neck."

Tidyman put his hands flat on the desk and leaned in towards me, his caterpillar eyebrows no longer awnings but now forming a black V. He looked like an enraged muppet.

"Because three people are dead that you knew. And you saw these people hours before they ended up dead. Those are coincidences I don't like because there is no such thing as coincidence," He was angry now and I felt like maybe I had pushed him a little too far. "Just because there's some calls from some other phones and you got some bullshit alibis doesn't mean you didn't have anything to do with this. You are fucking neck deep in this shit, Farrar. You either got something to do with it or you're holding out on us. Until you come clean, we're gonna be on your ass."

Himes looked at me then Tidyman and then back to me. We all sat unmoving and staring at each other until I took a breath.

"I did not kill those people," I said quietly. "I don't know who killed those people. I want to find out as much as you do, believe me. But your wasting time badgering me when there is a real killer out there. Now, are you charging me with something?"

Tidyman sucked his teeth and leaned back in his chair, setting off another squeal of protest. "Fucking cop shows. Everybody is a Goddamn lawyer now, like this is *Law And Order*. Fuck." Then he calmed himself and let out a long, drawn out breath.

"No. No, we are not charging you."

"Well," I said, rising and stretching out my lower back. My ass felt like I had been sitting on an engine block. "I am going then. Anything else I can help you with, feel free to call."

I started to turn but Tidyman said "Farrar."

"Yeah?"

"If you are holding back anything… anything… we're gonna find out," he said. He looked all business, his hands folded on his desk, his face serious but not angry. Just straightforward and no joke. "And you can end up going down for three murders as an accomplice. Three. That's just as bad as being the killer. So if you want to make it easier on yourself, give us the whole story now."

"I gave you the whole story. That's all I got." I said and started to leave.

There's an episode of *The Odd Couple* where Felix is

snowed in at a ski lodge during a photo shoot but no one knows where he is. Somehow this leads everybody to think that Oscar did away with him. At one point Oscar is at a police station getting grilled by this detective. Finally the cop tells Oscar he can go and walks out of the interrogation room. Oscar turns to Murray the cop and says, "Well, it can't be too bad. He didn't tell me to not leave town." Just then the cop sticks his head back in the room and says "Madison! Don't leave town!"

On that long walk from the desk to the elevator I half expected Tidyman to yell out "Farrar! Don't leave town!" But he never did and I got the hell out of there as fast as I possibly could without running.

14

I got in my Jeep, drove three blocks through the rain and then parked in front of somebody's house and just breathed. This had become insane. Three people had died and somehow I was a suspect. And it all seemed to tie in to a Superman piece of comic art. I had no idea where to find the art and exactly why it had led to so many killings, if in fact it had. It wasn't THAT valuable. Was it?

I was just sitting there staring at my windshield wipers when a man a few houses down from where I was parked walked out onto his porch smoking a cigarette. I see so many people having to do that now. The spouse doesn't want smoking in the house, complaining about the smell getting into everything. Can't say that I blame them. I smoked exactly once in my life and definitely was not a fan. The man smoked for a few minutes, protected from the weather by his porch awning and then pulled out his cellphone. A bell went off in my head. Right. Somebody had left a message on my phone. Ugh. I really, really didn't want to hear what glorious news possibly awaited me. Mr. Farrar, this is the Los Angeles police department. We'd like to ask you some questions concerning the Manson killings. Jesus. I sighed, sat back in the seat and reluctantly retrieved my message.

"Hello, William," the message started. "it's Mrs. Tang. Ken's mother. Or Poon, as you guys called him. I know all about that." Then she laughed. I covered my face and groaned. Her knowing that just made it a hundred times worse.

"Thank you so much for your message," Mrs. Tang continued. Her Chinese accent wasn't really heavy but you heard it clearly. She had a nice, light voice. She sounded so pleasant and energetic even after losing her son. Admirable. "Ken really liked you. I did, too. You loaned Ken three hundred dollars once and you didn't make a big deal out of it or anything. I thought that was really sweet of you."

I had completely forgotten about that. A few years back we were at a con in the Bronx and Poon really wanted this Gil Kane *Amazing Spider-man* page but had pretty much tapped himself out buying other stuff and was just short. I loaned him the money. I forgot his mom was there. Come to think of it, I'm not sure Poon ever paid me back. We probably worked it out somehow.

"I really appreciate you calling. I am so sad about Ken. Hearing from somebody like you is very nice. If you want to call back the number is 718 555-8273. Bye-bye."

I hung up from my voicemail line and thought about it while I listened to the rain. Should I really call up this poor woman and ask about some stupid comic page? It wasn't that stupid, though. I believed that it tied into three murders and possibly four. I had to ask about it. But I had to go easy. Mrs. Tang was dealing with her own devastating loss. She really didn't need to be bothered with this.

As I was weighing those opinions the guy who was smoking and talking on his porch hung up his phone and leaned against his wrought iron railing. He shook his head and took a long drag from his cigarette. Probably having a hard time with something, too. He stared across the street for a second, then took one last puff, tossed the cigarette into the gutter and took his phone back out. He seemed a lot more sure about what he wanted to do. So was I.

Mrs. Tang answered on the third rang and seemed actually pleased to be hearing back from me. I asked if she needed any help with anything.

"Oh, no, thank you, William. That's very sweet. I'm actually at Ken's apartment now, cleaning up. I have until the end of the month to pack everything together but I want to get as much done as early as possible. It's hard, you know?"

"I'm sure," I said, still not really knowing how to segue into my question. At least she was at Poon's apartment. Maybe that made it a little easier. "I'm really sorry. Ken was a good guy to know."

"Thank you, thank you."

"Um, Mrs. Tang?" I started. Might as well just go for it. "Have you come across a piece of Superman art while going through Ken's things? A cover? Somebody wants to buy it and Ken was supposedly the last to have it. I can describe it if you need."

"Actually there were three separate messages from a guy named Donnie asking about the same thing. He spoke very rudely. I think I met him once. I did not like him."

"Yeah, he.... he had that effect on people," I said. I didn't feel like explaining that Donnie was dead and it might've had to do with the art I was looking for. That was just too much.

"But, no. I haven't seen any Superman art. But then again I just started going through his things. You're welcome to come by and look if you like. Where are you?"

"I'm actually in Flushing. I had to run an errand out here." There was no way I was going to tell her I had just come from a police precinct. "I'm on 43rd Avenue."

"Oh, you're actually not too far from here. Do you have a pen?"

"Hold on," I said and fumbled through my glove compartment until I found a pen that actually wrote and an old envelope to write on. "Go ahead."

"I'm at 41-45 67 St. in Woodside. Apartment 4C. I think I can tell you how to get here from where you are."

"It's ok," I said, tossing the pen and envelope back into the glove compartment. I could easily remember that. "I'll find it on my phone. It'll actually call out directions."

"Oh!" she said, surprised. It always amused me to see how amazed older people were by technology. Yeah, so, if you click on this button it will send this text you just wrote to this person.

Oh!

"Thank you for inviting me," I said. "I don't want to be in your way… I know it's a difficult time."

"Don't worry about it. Look for the page. Maybe you'll find it. I don't think Ken ever paid you back that money. It's the least I could do."

"Well, thank you. I should be there in a few."

She said goodbye and we hung up and I typed in her address into my Apple GPS. Sure enough, she was very close by. About two miles. I put the phone in my cup holder and let it bark out instructions at me as I drove off.

It was still raining but nowhere near as hard as it had been earlier. It was more of a drizzle now but it remained pretty constant, keeping the wipers in business. Even if it stopped the sun would probably never crack through the thick gray ceiling that hung overhead. Though it was still cool it felt like it had gotten maybe a little warmer. Hopefully the system would pass through soon and there would be a return to bright, clear weather. I liked the rain but coupled with all of the bad stuff happening it was seriously killing my mood. For lack of a better phrase.

I hung a right on Hampton Street and cruised by a bunch of brick row houses and small apartment buildings. There weren't a lot of people out but most people were probably at work. If they weren't at work the rain was keeping them indoors and, hopefully, out of trouble. Although there were tons of trouble to get into indoors, apparently.

After that I made another right on Baxter and then a quick left onto Roosevelt Avenue, right under the elevated line where the 7 train ran. This part I knew or at least had seen on my way to Shea Stadium and now Citi Field to watch the Mets. I had never viewed it from street level before. There were tons of stores and a lot of traffic despite the rain. Now I knew where everybody was. Between the cabs, buses, trucks, vans and pedestrians it seemed like half of Queens was here.

Finally I made it to 67th Street, turned left and went a block before I saw my destination or more accurately the phone yelled at me that I had reached it. I found a spot across the street, parked and got out.

The building Poon lived in or used to live in was pretty nice. It had been refaced recently and all the windows appeared to have been replaced. New air conditioners jutted out of specially made slots and little balconies had been put in. It was only a four-story building but the balconies were probably nice to have anyway, especially on a cool spring evening. The front door was a clean stainless steel job with a black awning over it. Very, very cool looking. It definitely one upped my place of residence. Now if somebody could pick it up out of Queens and plant it somewhere in Brooklyn we would be getting somewhere.

There was a narrow space between the building and the one next to it. A black six-foot wrought iron gate was at the entrance of the narrow alley but it was closed and any visual through the bars was obscured by silver sheet metal that was pinned to the gate. I wondered if that was the alley that poor Poon fell into it. No wonder he wasn't found for a while. I shuddered and went to the front door.

After I shook off the rain and thumbed the button for apartment 4C I was buzzed in and I hopped onto the elevator. The elevator was also refaced and well taken care of. Shiny new buttons, new tiled floor. I was impressed with this building. Still not impressed enough to move to Queens but that's just me.

Mrs. Tang was standing outside the apartment door when I stepped off of the elevator. She was just as I remembered her. Very short, at least 5′ 1″, very slim, attractive and probably much younger looking than she was. She always had a perpetual smile it seemed and this time was no exception. She wore loose fitting jeans and a pink sweatshirt with the sleeves rolled up. Her hair was back in a ponytail but some of it was hanging down the either side of her round face. She looked like she had been working.

I went to shake her hand but she hugged me and I hugged her back. She seemed like she needed one. Or maybe I did. Then she invited me in.

It was a nice little apartment. Through the front door led to a nice living room like mine but the kitchen was off to the right as opposed to being on the left for me. It was larger, too. And it had a cut out so you could see into the living room while you were cooking or whatever. The living room was larger than mine as well, which Poon had decorated much like mine. He was a bigger Star Wars fan than I was, though so his posters were mostly Drew Struzan prints of the original trilogy and the Special Edition releases. I idly wondered if he had the prequel posters. Probably in the bathroom, I thought, which amused me.

There was a little hall to my left where I caught a glimpse of bedroom and a look at the bathroom which was at the end. The bathroom was bigger than mine, too. This building was starting to get on my nerves.

"I really appreciate you letting me come over, Mrs. Tang," I said, taking off my wet hoodie. "I know you're busy."

"It's no problem at all," she said, taking my hoodie and laying over a stool. She went into the kitchen and I saw moving boxes filled with dishware and pots and pans sitting on the floor and the counter. There was also glassware, lots and lots of glassware. Counting mugs I had maybe eight glasses in my entire apartment and one of them was cracked. I don't know why I kept it. Here there were dozens and dozens of different types of flutes, mugs, shot glasses, juice glasses, wine glasses, you name it. Wow. Poon must've had a real thing about glassware. "Honestly, it's nice to have someone else here. It's too quiet and I don't want to hear the TV or radio."

"Do you need any help?"

"No, no," she said, picking up one of the army of glass and wrapping it in newspaper. "I'm ok. Keeping busy. Ken kept a lot of his comic art in the bedroom. There's a flat file in the closet. Look in there and see if you can find what you need."

I went into the bedroom and looked around. There were two windows furthest from the door that looked out onto the backyards of houses behind the building. In the wall to the left of those was a smaller window. I pulled up the blinds and peered out. It looked down into the little alley that I assume Poon had fallen into. There was the other building next door but luckily there were no windows facing this one. Seemed like an odd little window to be cleaning and to accidentally fall out of. I had to believe with all that had happened that this was no accident.

I dropped the blinds back down and then checked out the walls. They all had framed comic art on them, at least 30 pieces. Poon and Chandler made me feel like a real newbie. I looked at each one but there was no Swan cover for a Superman. That would've been too easy. Besides if Poon had been pushed whoever had done it would've seen it. There were no empty spots either. I took a few minutes to enjoy the art, though. There were two John Romita *Spider-man* newspaper comic strips, one being a Sunday. Those weren't easy to get a hold of. There was a Johnny Craig piece from one of those crazy EC horror books from the 50's like *Vault Of Horror* or *Tales From The Crypt*. Really nice. There was a great Steve Rude painted *Nexus* cover. Next to that were two John Buscema *Avengers* pages, a Gil Kane page from *What If* #3 that was amazing and a two page spread of a Mort Drucker *MAD* spoof of *Superman: The Movie* that was pure genius. I didn't want to be staring at these things all day so I did a quick check and then moved to the closet. I was already feeling like a vulture and now I was thinking of asking Mrs. Tang if she would like to sell some of them to me. Jeez, Will, Poon's body was still warm. Give it a minute.

The closet was a walk in type that was a pretty good size. On the right were shelves at eye level with shirts and sweaters and underneath a pole that had pants on hangers. Straight in the back was a black flat file that wasn't very wide but tall with about ten drawers. I started at the top.

There were far too many great pieces of art in that flat file to list, far too many that I wanted to run out of the apartment with. But none of them were the Superman cover. I searched the whole room, under the bed and dresser, behind the art that was hanging and nothing. With Mrs. Tang's permission I searched the rest of the apartment as well. All through the living room, the hall closet, the cabinets in the kitchen, everywhere. The Superman cover was, I was pretty sure, not in this house.

I wandered back to the kitchen and leaned against the door frame.

"I've looked everywhere. I don't think it's here."

Mrs. Tang was folding up another moving box. She stopped and gave me genuine sad face. "I'm sorry! I know you really wanted to find it. Someone wants it badly, I guess, huh?"

Uh... yeah. Definitely." I stood there and looked around the apartment again, as if there would be a secret hiding place that would suddenly become apparent. "Damn."

"Well, have a seat for a minute and give it some more thought. Maybe you'll come up with another idea." said

Mrs. Tang, now in full mom mode. She probably really missed mothering someone.

I sighed and dragged myself to the couch in the living room and dropped onto it. Here I was again at a complete standstill. I didn't know where else to look. I thought back on my steps and then took out my phone and scanned my contacts. I remembered the three people outside of the city I wanted to get in touch with but I didn't really have high hopes about them. They were kind of out of the loop and I just didn't have a good feeling about them shedding any light on this mystery. I was getting depressed because I felt like I had run out of gas on my search and I would never find out what the big deal was. I'd never find out why people died over it.

I slumped further on the couch and looked again at the boxes that littered the apartment, some full, most not, a lot still waiting to be built. They all had a logo for Woodside Storage on the side, a drawing of a big, green W on the side of a moving box and the name in an arch above with the address in an arch below. But the logos were different on some. I was bored and annoyed but I didn't have anything better to do so I looked closer at one of the boxes and then compared it to another. One of the logos looked older, like it was designed a long time ago. And the other was cleaner, more modern, with more subtle colors. A different typeface, too. They had updated the logo. Were they still selling off the boxes with the older art? I wondered how many boxes they had left with the old logo on them. God knows how many. I wondered if most people even noticed the difference. I wondered why I was even wondering about this nonsense.

Then I started looking closer at the boxes themselves. They looked the same mostly but a few with the old logos were a little dog-eared, like they had been sitting around for a while. That got my attention and got the little wheels in my brain moving again. Had these boxes been at the storage place all this time? Or had Ken bought them awhile back?

"Mrs. Tang, did you just buy these boxes? The older ones? These ones that are a little dog-eared?"

Mrs. Tang put down another glass that she had wrapped in newspaper and squinted in my direction. "Oh no, Ken had some of them in the storage unit already. He probably bought something in and just left them in there. I just brought those back with me."

A storage unit. Poon had a storage unit.

"So, this unit...." I said, trying hard to sound casual, "he's had it for awhile?"

"Oh, probably for a couple of years now. He always left the keys with me since we lived so close to one another. Ken didn't want anyone to know he had one." She stopped and looked around, lowering her voice to a whisper, like somebody was just outside the door. "He didn't trust a lot of the comic book people you know." Then a lightbulb seemed to come on over her head. "Oh! Maybe that comic page you're looking for is in there?"

"Hmm! Maybe!" I said, acting stupid. "That's a possibility." I really needed to get over there but felt crappy about bugging a grieving mother to take me there. I was already being a pain, I felt like, but I didn't have any choice. I had to get to the bottom of this.

"Um... I'm sorry, Mrs. Tang," I started, struggling to phrase this as gently as I could. "I know you're busy now but maybe if you have a few minutes we could...?"

Mrs. Tang walked over to the counter and picked up a set of keys. Four of the keys had little red plastic covers over the ends that said Woodside Storage. She dropped the whole set into my hand.

"You go ahead. It's only a little ways from here."

I put the keys down on the counter and stepped back. "No. I'd rather you go with me. I don't want to fumble through Ken's stuff without you being there."

Mrs. Tang put more wrapped glasses in a box. "You go over and look. Come back and show me what you have." She smiled up at me. "I trust you."

"I'll pay you for it. That's fair." I felt shitty saying fair. If it was there I was going to make a few grand off of this thing.

"Don't worry about it." said Mrs. Tang. "Ken owed you. Go over and see." She smiled and dangled the keys enticingly. "Maybe you'll luck out."

15

Woodside Storage was about two and a half miles from Poon's apartment and sat just above the BQE, which ran in a trench in this part of Queens about 20 feet down from street level. It was a brick two-story building that, oddly enough, was on the same land as a cemetery, which was a completely different type of storage. There were a few signs of this being a very old building - some sort of warehouse or factory many years ago - but now it looked fairly modern with fresh paint and redone loading docks. I guess the logo wasn't the only thing that had been updated.

Though it was only two stories it made up for its lack of height with a great deal of width. The building was quite sprawling with what appeared to be an addition added recently. Even though it was early afternoon there were a fair amount of people moving stuff in and out on carts and hand trucks. U-Haul vans and other vehicles were either parked in the lot or in the loading bays getting filled or unpacked. I pulled into an empty spot on the far end of the lot, got out and took in the scene. Man, people had a lot of stuff. Who was I kidding, I had my own little storage unit in Brooklyn. We all had a lot of stuff that we didn't know what to do with.

It had stopped raining so that saved people the annoyance of having to throw a tarp over their items. It wasn't just boxes that were being brought in or out. There were beds and chairs and TV's and couches and bookcases and all manner of stuff being moved. Silly me, I showed up empty handed. Hopefully I wouldn't be leaving that way.

Mrs. Tang had told me that I could just walk in and get on the elevator without being anywhere near the main office but I still felt like I was doing something wrong. I don't know why. I had Mrs. Tang's blessings and keys so I was good. It wasn't like I was robbing the joint.

I went up a set of stairs next to a loading dock where two guys were dragging a heavy looking treadmill out of a van and headed over to the elevator. Poon's unit was number 2395 and I had four different keys with a Woodside Storage marker on them. I had just noticed that. I guess I would get my explanation as to why when I got to it.

I should've found the stairs because there was a husband and wife with a cart full of boxes and clothes and all kinds of stuff that were arguing as they waited for the elevator. Apparently there was some disagreement as to how many trips they needed to make and how many they wanted to. They were pretty nasty to one another and every time they even slightly shifted the cart something would fall off. Eventually the elevator came and they pushed the cart in, arguing and dropping stuff the entire time. When we got to two it took them at least five minutes to get off of the elevator as they were going at each other and picking up their crap. They were so consumed with their fighting that I don't think they even noticed me. Or cared. Luckily they went the opposite direction that I needed to. If I had to listen to those two the whole time I would kill myself.

The place was a labyrinth made out of cinder blocks and aluminum. I swear, those numbers weren't in any kind of order that I could decipher but I finally found Poon's spot, which sat almost at the end of one of the corridors. No one was in the aisle but me and it was amazingly quiet. I couldn't hear the moving lovebirds or anyone else for that matter. Nice.

I realized why there were four different keys when I saw the unit because there were four different locks. Four locks, a unit tucked away in the back, a unit number that wasn't written down anywhere and only your mom with the keys. Poon wasn't messing around. He was all Secret Squirrel with this bad boy. I finally figured out which key went with each lock and pulled the gate up.

Poon looked like he had a ten-foot by ten-foot unit like I did but where mine was generally a haphazard mess, his was neat, efficiently arranged and orderly. The way his apartment looked should have been a clue. There were two black shelving units each against the left and right walls holding long white comic book boxes and two stacked flat files, similar to the one Poon had at home against the back wall facing the gate. There were more longboxes on top of the flat files. I opened the lid on one and thumbed through a bunch of *Tom Strong* comics by Alan Moore and Chris Sprouse. I went further and there were *Top Ten* issues by Moore and Gene Ha. Both of these were great books. I started to pull out a *Tom Strong* I didn't have, caught myself and put it back, closing the white cardboard box lid. I would be here until doomsday if got caught up in some comics. Had to stay on task.

I opened the first draw of the top flat file and pulled out comic art. A Stuart Immonen *All-New X-Men* page, an old Gene Colan *Iron Man* page, an Ed McGuinness *Superman/Batman*… there was a goldmine in here. I carefully took each page out and put them aside. I would ask Mrs. Tang if she were interested in selling this art. I could definitely move these pieces. Shoot, I might buy half of them myself.

I was about halfway through the second drawer when I heard a noise in the hall. I peeked out and about four units down a little, heavy set older guy in a black Adidas track suit was pulling a rack of Sheepskin coats out of his space. He caught sight of me and looked momentarily confused.

"Oh. Hello," he said.

"Hi," I said and set down a box with art on it into the hall. I was running out of space to move inside. When I looked back up Adidas guy was still staring at me. I waved and went back into the unit.

I knew exactly what was going to happen next. Just had to wait. Sure enough, a minute or two later Adidas guy came down and stuck his balding head in.

"Hi! How are you?"

I rolled my eyes before I turned to face him. "Not bad. How are you?"

"Ok," he said, fiddling with his glasses. He struggled to find a follow up question and then settled on "Busy, huh?"

"Yeah. Trying to find something and having a little trouble."

"Oh," he said. Then he tried to get slick. "Helping out

Mike and his dad?"

I put down a George Perez page from an old issue of *The New Teen Titans* that I once had and said "Mike? You must mean Ken, right? Ken Tang. And not his dad but his mother."

That really put Adidas guy on his heels. "Oh yeah, right. Got the name wrong."

"Ok," I said. "Well, Mrs. Tang gave me the keys and told me to look for what I needed. We can call her if you like? If you need confirmation or something."

Adidas guy turned beet red and put his hands up. "I wasn't…' he stammered. "I didn't mean to make it sound like…"

He put his hands down and looked at me. I looked back. I wasn't giving him an out.

"Sorry. I wasn't accusing you of anything."

"Ok. Just in case you were wondering."

"Ok." Adidas guy looked mortified and at a complete loss as to what to say next. Finally he gave me a little wave and said, "Well… I'll, um… let you get back to work."

"Ok," I said and watched him go. A few years ago I saw a video where they chained a bike to a metal sign in a park, had a white kid try and steal it and then a black kid do the same thing. Passersby were practically helping the white kid steal the bike. He's hacking at the chain and basically telling people it wasn't his but no one did anything. Finally after an hour some old couple sort of threatened to get somebody. When the black kid did it he damn near got lynched immediately. So as I watched Adidas guy walk away I wondered if he would've done the same thing if I were a white dude. That annoyed me. Plus, he was wearing a pair of Nike Air Max's with an Adidas tracksuit. Shameful.

I looked through and emptied each drawer in the flat files and saw some great art but none of it was the one I needed. I decided to go through them again and briefly thought about getting a pen and pad and cataloguing it all. But that would just be busy work. Job number one was finding that art and I was failing at it. While I was going through it again Adidas guy came over and asked if I wanted something from outside. Trying to make amends. I should've made him get me a Pepsi but I just wanted him to leave me alone. I was annoyed enough already.

After I did my second trip through the art and put it all back I sat on the floor in the corner and just stared at the flat files. I had to really face the possibility that Poon never had this art at all. But why had he been so elusive and vague with Donnie when he was asked about it? Why had he misled him with some bad info? Apparently Donnie hadn't been the only one that Poon told that story to. Michael Rothstein had gotten a couple of calls concerning it. So it wasn't crazy for me to think that Poon had this art. He had already shown that he would go to some great lengths to hide something. I went back downstairs, got my little LED flashlight out of the glove compartment and came back up ready to search everywhere. I was starting to get hungry but that could wait.

I looked behind and under the metal shelving units and was about to look behind the flat files when I noticed that they were not sitting directly on the floor. They were resting on what looked like one inch by one-inch strips of dark wood that ran the width of the flat files, one at the front end and one at the back. Maybe Poon was concerned about a busted water pipe or damage from sprinklers or something. I would be too so I could understand raising them. There was a slot of space between the two slats of wood on either side so I got down in the narrow space next to it and looked in with the flashlight. I saw what looked like a long, flat, brown cardboard box and started getting excited. Then I told myself to calm down and tried to figure out how to reach it. It was way too small a space to get my hands in there. I went around to the other side but couldn't reach it from there, either. I didn't have a stick or a rod or anything and was just about to head back down to the Jeep for something when it occurred to me that I could unfold one of the long comic box tops and maybe use that. Once I took the sides of the lid out of their tabs it was just a long flat piece of cardboard. I slid it under the flat files until it pushed the box out.

The box was maybe two feet by three feet with no markings on it and little folded in flaps at either end that were taped. I pulled at it but it was really tough ass tape. Damn, Poon. You would think the Declaration of Independence was in here. Maybe it was.

Without having to run out to get a light saber I actually managed to rip the tape away from the box. The tape itself never tore, though. Wow. I decided to replace my Master locks at my storage unit with this stuff. You would die trying to get through it.

Before I opened the box I stuck my head out and peeked down the hall. Adidas guy had three more racks of coats out and was counting and checking off a piece of paper he was holding. Inventory. I went back over to the box, unfolded the flap and slowly pulled out what was inside.

It was a flat, really hard, black metal box and for a few stupid moments it did not occur to me that I was looking at the back of it. I slowly turned it over and it was a frame and inside the frame in all his black and white glory was Superman.

He was actually changing from Clark Kent to Superman, holding his glasses in his left hand and pulling off his shirt, tie and jacket with his right. No doubt heading off to save someone, probably Lois. In the foreground three criminals watched through a trick mirror and laughed over finally knowing Superman's secret identity. One held a box with gold Kryptonite in it. It was the cover I saw online but a scanned lo-res jpeg of a cover printed in 1963 couldn't hope to do justice to what I held in my hands now. The word balloons were peeling and there was a yellowish rubber cement stain near the *Action Comics* masthead and white paint covering up all the smudges and mistakes and despite all of that it was beautiful, absolutely beautiful. It was a classic piece of comic art. I vowed to look at the body of Curt Swan's work again and to fully appreciate his talent.

But it still didn't explain why people had gone to such great lengths to find it. It was a lovely piece, definitely great to own but certainly not worth killing for. There were no signatures or anything, none that I could see, anyway. Maybe something was on the back? I fumbled around the edges of the frame, trying to figure out how to open it. And that's when I noticed the little combination lock.

It was like the kind that briefcases have, with the little dials that spin but it was just one set and one lock. There were six dials of numbers and it was all black and almost flush to the bottom of the frame. If it were hanging on a wall you wouldn't even notice it. It was definitely a custom made job, I had never seen one like this before. And even if it wasn't custom made it was expensive. I tapped on the pane of Plexiglas over the art in the frame but you could tell it was tough and durable. You would have to destroy the art to get it out.

I turned the frame back over to the combination lock and stared at it. This was getting ridiculous. All the secrecy and security that went into this thing… I couldn't blame Poon for keeping it. He knew there was a whole lot more to this and just had to find a way to get it open without ruining the art. He just didn't know how badly somebody wanted it. And he probably paid for it. I wanted to know what the deal was too before I turned it over to Chandler. But what was the combination?

I tried different combinations of digits using the issue number, 305, the cover month, 10 and the year of publication, 1963. Of course none of them worked. Why would you use a set of numbers for a lock that were clearly visible on the item itself? Stupid. These could be any numbers. Numbers that meant something only to Coleman Chandler and Steve Carvell. How would I even guess?

When it hit me it was like a physical thing and I almost dropped the frame. The numbers. The numbers on the little sheet of paper that Chandler tried to hide from me in his art room. No. No way. Maybe? But I couldn't remember them. Try as I might I couldn't and then I realized that my mind was racing too fast and I just needed to calm down and remember. Just slow it all down and remember.

There was an X-acto blade, a black matte frame and a John Romita Spider-man page on the flat file. I had sneakily hidden my cell under the Romita art. Chandler dropped the sheet of paper into a little drawer on the right side of the flat file so I opened the drawer and took the paper out and unfolded it and the paper said....

48, 49 and 50.

Yes, that was it. Those were the numbers.

I carefully dialed the numbers into the six positions and found a little notch on the other end of the frame and slowly pulled.

The frame opened.

I put my fingers in the opening so it wouldn't close, went back to the door and stuck my head out again. Adidas guy was still deep in his inventory, this time with his back to me. Good. I went as far back in the unit as I could and opened the frame. It swung easily and the black matte came with it.

The art somehow looked even better than it had before. Probably only because I could actually get my hands on it. I took it out flipped it over.

Nothing.

I sighed and leaned against the wall, shaking my head. I didn't get any of this. Then I glanced into the metal frame.

There was a sheet of paper still in it the same size as the Superman art. It was thin and not entirely opaque.

I could see something underneath it.

I pulled up the thin sheet and probably for the next minute or so gawked at what was underneath. I couldn't wrap my brain around it. Not because I didn't know what it was but because I couldn't believe it was here. And real. I slowly lifted it out of the frame and blinked at it.

It was the cover to *Fantastic Four* number 48, a classic issue in a classic run of them. But this one was very special. On it Mr. Fantastic (Reed Richards), The Invisible Girl (Sue Storm, his wife), the Human Torch (Johnny Storm, Sue's little brother), the Thing (Ben Grimm, Reed's longtime friend) and a crowd of people were looking fearfully past the viewer and up into the sky. Next to them stood The Watcher, a giant, robed alien who watched over the cosmos and appeared at critical moments in history. Above the F.F. the blurb yelled "The Coming Of Galactus!" It would be the first appearance of Galactus, the Devourer of Worlds and his herald, The Silver Surfer, longtime popular characters and mainstays in the Marvel Universe. The Fantastic Four was, in a lot of ways, the hub that the Marvel Universe spiraled out from. So many popular characters and concepts and worlds started in that book and built the foundation that Marvel rested on. For one hundred issues Stan (The Man)

Lee and Jack (King) Kirby did the book and this was right smack dab in the middle of their run and at the height of their powers. And here I was holding this landmark cover in my hands.

It was a true, undeniable work of art. Inked by the great Joe Sinnott, it leapt out at you, even with a static shot of characters looking into the sky. Nothing was static when Jack Kirby drew it.

The art was in pristine condition. The masthead and type were on perfectly and the board was a light, even color. I'd never held anything like that in my hands before.

Well, to state the obvious, it seemed that Coleman Chandler had been a little less than forthcoming about the entire contents of this item. Now it all made sense: the need to find this art, to stop others from retrieving it first… and to actually kill for it. There was no telling what a person could get for this cover. Definitely over fifty grand. Easily.

I was leaning against the flat file with the frame behind me when I was struck again by a realization that actually jarred me. Why had the numbers been 48, 49 and 50? No. No, it couldn't be. I looked back in the frame and there was another translucent sheet of paper. I lifted it and took out was underneath.

Sure enough it was the cover to *Fantastic Four* #49, an even better known cover than #48 and oft copied. On it

Reed, Sue, Ben and Johnny were racing towards the viewer, dodging destructive blasts of energy from the hands of Galactus. Between the helmeted giant alien's hands flew the Silver Surfer, watching the F.F. flee. If you thought Kirby could knock it out of the park with a cover of people just standing around staring into the sky then you would be blown away by this piece. Another classic, clean ink job by Sinnott with a blurb that yelled "If This Be Doomsday!". This piece was in fantastic shape as well. It was even more valuable than the #48 cover, way more. This was the very first cover that Galactus and the Surfer ever appeared on. I wouldn't begin to put a price on it. Collectors would just throw suitcases full of money at you for it.

I put that one down and looked again into the frame. Another sheet of paper. Underneath I expected to see the cover to number #50, which had the main shot of the Surfer riding his board with the floating heads of the Reed, Ben and Sue. On the bottom right was a shot of Johnny out of costume and on campus as the blurb yelled something about Johnny heading to college. That's what I expected to see but that isn't what I got. When I pulled it out I saw that it was actually the splash page to that issue, which was even better than the cover.

Under a banner that said "The Startling Saga Of The Silver Surfer", lettered beautifully by Sam Rosen, the Surfer flies in the foreground, pleading with Galactus to spare the earth. Below and to the right of Galactus, Reed, Sue and Ben are trapped in a force field. If you know F.F. history, you know that Johnny has been dispatched by the Watcher to retrieve the one weapon that can stop Galactus: the Ultimate Nullifier. Below them were the credits for the issue. Again, Lee, Kirby, Sinnott and Rosen were the folks behind this gem.

Much like the other pieces this one too was in impeccable condition, clean, no, scratches or frayed edges. And the fact that it was a splash page from a groundbreaking issue with two classic characters on it besides the main heroes made it possibly worth more than the others. I didn't want to think about what I could sell the three pieces for. This would easily, easily bring in the most money I had ever seen in my life. It was like winning the lottery.

I thought seriously about getting the police involved. Bringing the frame and everything inside to Tidyman and Himes and just being done with it. But there was still no concrete, solid proof that this art was what got killed four people killed. I believed it was but I also believed in Santa Claus when I was a kid. Just because I thought so it didn't make it gospel. Besides, regardless of Chandler covering it up, this artwork was legally, as far as I knew, his. And there was the little matter of the three grand Chandler owed me for finding this. I'm a nice guy if I do say so myself but I was gonna push for more. This search had been way over the normal aggravation level these things normally are. Add to that the value of the hidden art and I thought I definitely needed a good bonus. Not that I was supposed to be aware of the Kirby art. But I would let Chandler know that I figured out what he was hiding without going into details. Make a little extra dough and get the hell out of this craziness.

I put the art back, all of it, exactly as I found it, closed up the frame and slipped it back into the cardboard box. Then I straightened up the storage unit, pulled the gate down and put all the locks back on. Adidas guy was drinking a soda and watched me as I went by. He was probably dying to know what was in the box I was carrying. I waved and found my way to the elevator.

When I got inside the Jeep I called Mrs. Tang and told her I found what I had been looking for and would be dropping the keys off. I also told her that I would give her two thousand dollars for the art. She fought me on it, hard, but I convinced her to take it. At least, I thought I did. Who knows what kind of fight we would have when I actually tried to give it to her. Then I called Jessica.

"I found it," I said after she had answered. There was silence for a second and then when she answered she sounded all manner of confused.

"You found... wait. Wait," she stammered. "You found IT? You mean, you found the Superman art? The actual art?"

"Yup."

"Oh, my God. I can't believe it. Where? How?"

"I'll explain that later. Is Mr. Chandler home?"

There was a pause. "Um... yeah. I'm sure he is. He didn't tell me he was going anywhere."

"Ok. I'll be over in about an hour. Maybe a little more."

There was another pause and then she said, "Let me meet you somewhere. I want to verify it."

Now it was my turn to pause. What? "It's the art, Jessica. I know it is. I'll be over in a bit. Tell him I'm coming."

"Wait. Don't come here. Meet me... meet me outside your place. Wait in your Jeep for me. I can be there in less time than it will take for you to get here."

"Listen to me," I said, trying not to get angry. "Listen. Now, I don't know what the hell is going on with you and I don't know what's going on with all the crazy shit about this cover. But your father hired me to find this. I have found it and I am bringing it directly to him. I'm not meeting you at my place or on the street or in Grand Central Station at fucking midnight, Jessica. I am giving it to him and then I want my money and then I am going to forget about you and all this crazy business because I've had it with this shit. I want my money and then I am done. Do you understand what I am saying?"

She was quiet again for a long time, so long that for a second I thought she had hung up. But then she said quietly but firmly, "Fine. Come here, then. We'll be waiting for you." Then she hung up.

I sat there for a bit and thought about her reaction. I didn't understand it. I didn't understand any of it. I thought briefly again about going to the police but I talked myself out of it. What would I even say?

It was 3:07 and I still hadn't eaten yet. I could drop by Mrs. Tang, grab a bite and get to Chandler's long before sundown. I didn't know why that was important, to be there before sundown. This thing was putting stupid thoughts in my head. I just wanted it to be over with.

I put the Jeep into drive and left.

One hour and twenty-two minutes, a short trip back to Mrs. Tang's and five White Castle double cheeseburgers later (I know, I know, I would live to regret those), I was pulling up to the silver callbox again at Coleman Chandler's house. Again there was no voice but just a buzz and the gates slowly and silently moved open. I followed the drive up to the garage and saw that beautiful Bentley Mulsanne, gleaming in the sun that had somehow managed to crawl out from behind the clouds about an hour previous. At least the day would end nicely. But in addition to the Bentley there were both Audi R8's parked this time, the silver one and the black one. Someone would have to tell Jessica that you can only drive one car at a time. A sad but true fact.

I parked and got out, retrieving my cardboard box from the back seat. Above the house gliding on the gentle breeze were two hawks, both with incredible wingspans. They seemed to just hang there for a second and then floated towards the trees beyond the back of the house. They looked so beautiful, so at peace. Serene. Well, at least that's what I thought. A rabbit may think otherwise.

When I got to the door, Jessica was waiting for me. She was wearing tight darks jeans with black short boots and the same black jacket she wore to my apartment with a gray blouse underneath. She also wore a pretty serious looking scowl until she saw the box in my hands. Then there was a small smile but not a very pretty one. Even with the half-hearted attempt at niceness she still looked pretty hot. I wasn't going to linger on that, though. That was definitely a thing of the past. Drop off the artwork, get my money and never look back. Being polite I still said hi but got back a pretty cold hello. Whatever.

"Dad's upstairs," she said and motioned into the house. I went through the giant foyer, glanced again at the picture of her mother and her aunt and then to the stairs. Jessica followed, silent. I didn't try to make small talk. What would be the point? I just climbed the two flights and walked into the gallery.

The first person I saw was Rick and I was more than a little stunned to see that he was holding what looked to be a Glock automatic. He glanced at me and smiled humorlessly and I felt an angry burn in my stomach. That sonuvabitch. I knew it. Then I felt like I was completely losing my mind because he was pointing the gun at Coleman Chandler and Jessica. She was dressed differently, wearing lighter jeans with a pink hoodie pullover and white Nikes but it was, impossibly, Jessica. How could that be? I turned to look back and there was the other Jessica pointing another gun towards me and then it all became suddenly clear. The real reason why she had visited me in Brooklyn. Why she hadn't told her father anything. The two different Audi's. The weird behavior. The misunderstandings on the phone. All of it.

And I thought of the picture downstairs of her mother and her aunt. So alike. You couldn't tell them apart.

"You're Jennifer," I said. "All this time you were

Jennifer."

She snorted and shook her head, a nasty little smirk on her face.

"You're a fucking genius, dude," she said. Then she laughed.

In hindsight I probably should've gone to the police.

16

"Can you please tell me what the hell this is all about?" said Coleman Chandler, to no one in particular. He was red-faced and angry, practically shaking. I was worried that he would pop a blood vessel. He pointed a quivering finger at Jennifer and gritted his teeth.

"I haven't seen or heard from you in months and then you come barging into my house with a gun?" Then Chandler looked at Rick and the anger fell away to sadness. "And you.... What are you doing? How can you do this? I gave you a life and a home."

"Shut up," said Rick, shaking his head. "I was just a gofer and a cab driver. You and my dad act like you did me this huge favor. So you gave me a place to live. So what? You still treat me like you own me. So just shut up."

Jennifer took the box from me and put it on the flat file desk.

"What is this?" said Chandler.

"It's what they wanted all along," I said. Rick herded me over to stand with Chandler and Jessica. She looked at me with wide, panicky eyes, absolutely terrified. That worried me. That said she was really frightened of what her sister could do. "Your art."

Jennifer opened the box and pulled out the sleek black frame. For a second she and Rick were mesmerized by it, not even paying attention to us. A brief thought of making a move skittered across my brain but I'm not the Rock. I couldn't try to disarm them both without getting me or Chandler or Jessica blasted. Then I saw the X-acto blade still on the desk. I palmed it quickly and dropped it into my pocket, point down.

Chandler eyes widened and then he composed somewhat and said, "The Superman art? But… it can't be worth that - "

"Stop it, Dad," said Jennifer. She put the frame down gently like it was the most valuable thing in the world. To her I guess it was. "You sound stupid. We know what's really in there."

Chandler's face fell. Jessica looked at him and then her

sister and back to her father. "What are they talking about? What does she mean?"

Jennifer laughed and waved the gun in Jessica's direction, who recoiled and grabbed her father's arm. "You didn't even know? This has got to be a first. I know something that Saint Jess doesn't? Amazing."

Jessica still looked confused so I said, "Your father had something more than that Superman art in there. Something extremely valuable."

Everyone looked at me with raised eyebrows, especially Chandler.

"Yes, I know about the Fantastic Four art," I said. "And Jennifer and Rick does, too. Rick probably overheard you speaking to Steve's widow about receiving the art in the will. So they arranged the little "break in" on the Bentley. Nothing to arrange, really. Rick just found a quiet spot and did it himself. He didn't know that you didn't trust him or Jessica or anybody with that art. So you had it hidden. And when he got the frame back to Jennifer they were surprised to the see the Superman art. A good prize but not nearly the jackpot they were hoping for."

"I've been looking at that art in Uncle Steve's stupid house since I was a little girl," said Jennifer, shaking her head. "Jess never paid any attention to it but I did. He used to talk about how valuable it was. When I heard dad was gonna get it I knew I could make a ton of money from it. I have three guys interested in it, no questions asked. Three rich geeks, all willing to pay top dollar for it. You wouldn't believe how much."

"This is all about money?" said Chandler. He took a step towards Jennifer but she leveled the gun at him and he stopped. The gun was still and steady and her face was hard. I couldn't believe how hard. "I can give you money, Jen. I'll write a check and you can take Rick and go. I won't stop you. Just promise to go and you can have all the money you want."

Jennifer stared at her father like she was thinking about it. Thinking hard. Then she looked at Rick, questioning. Rick shook his head angrily and hissed, "Don't be fuckin' stupid, Jen. You think daddy's gonna write you a check and let you just stroll out the fuckin' door? You wouldn't make it to South Orange Avenue before the cops scooped you up."

She still seemed on the fence, wavering. Then Rick stepped closer and drove in the final nail. "He cut you loose before. He stopped giving you money and kicked you out. Told you to make it on your own. Now suddenly he's gonna give you all the money you want? He's saving his own ass, Jen. We've come too far and done too many things to stop now. People died behind this shit. There's no walking away now."

Jessica took a step back but there wasn't any more room. She was wedged between her father and two John Byrne *Man of Steel* pages on the wall. I didn't think her eyes could get any wider than before but she proved me wrong. Besides her hairstyle and clothing I still could see no difference between her and her sister. It was amazing. I still felt like an idiot getting played like this, though.

"Oh my God," Jessica said quietly, like she really didn't want to say it. "You did kill those men that attacked William. Oh my God."

"They were making trouble," I said. "Even though they had no idea what they were involved in. Rick and your sister also killed my friend Ken Tang. After they thought they had the wrong art they sold it to Ken. Then nosy Rick probably listened in on you talking to Steve's widow again and he knew the truth. They went back to Ken but he knew he had something good so he lied to them. Sent them on a wild goose chase to a guy in Jersey. But they figured out that he was leading them on. So my guess is they tried to scare him into telling where the art was."

Jennifer sneered at Rick and I could tell it was his idea to dangle Poon out of a window. He gave her an angry, defensive look and then glared back at me.

"They didn't mean to kill him but that doesn't matter. He's still dead," I said. "And they did it."

"No," said Chandler. "No. This can't be. You told me these deaths were not connected. They couldn't have killed anyone. That's insane. That's.... no."

"They also killed Donnie Castiglia."

Both Chandler and Jessica looked at me in amazement. This must've been so hard to listen to, that your daughter and twin sister was a cold-blooded killer, a heartless murderer. I couldn't even imagine what that felt like.

"Yeah, he's dead. I found his body last night at his store. They got the drop on him and tortured him to death."

"Stupid fat fuck," said Jennifer. She laughed a little when she said it and I could finally see the difference in her and her sister. She was completely without morals and compassion and concern for other humans. It played out on her face. She made expressions that I don't think Jessica could if she tried.

"After he called dad and started making noise about knowing where the art was I called him. Didn't tell him who I was. He really thought we would show up when he said so," Jennifer laughed and shook her head. "What an asshole. I knew he really didn't have it but we had to know for sure."

"So you tried to get the truth out of him but he wouldn't talk... until you took it too far." I said.

Jennifer glanced at Rick again and snorted. "Next time I come up with the questioning techniques. This guy makes it hard for people to give you an answer."

"Shut up," said Rick quietly.

"No, YOU shut up!" yelled Jennifer. She shifted so quickly to anger that it startled me. "You fucked this whole thing up. You shut up and listen to ME."

Rick's face folded in and he turned red but he said nothing. It was clear who was in charge.

"But it looks like we don't have to question anyone else because you brought the art right to us," said Jennifer, calming again. I began to suspect that she was bipolar or something. Not that it really mattered now. "I knew you were the one to keep an eye on. I knew you could find it."

"Wow," I said. "You got all that by sleeping with me?"

Jennifer's eyes narrowed as she stared at me and her lips became a hard, straight line across her face. Yep, I was pretty sure I had just blown up her spot. I think she was considering shooting me but thought better of it. I didn't dare look at Chandler and Jessica. This was already the craziest family drama ever and I just dropped another bomb right in the middle of it. I didn't want to see their expressions but I was very interested in seeing Rick's. Admittedly, I was being a jackass but at this point all I had left were buttons to push.

Rick didn't disappoint. His eyes widened and his mouth fell open and he looked like somebody just ran over his dog.

"What? You slept with him?"

"It got us the art, didn't it?" said Jennifer, whirling to face him. "It didn't mean anything. Look what it got us."

"Jesus Christ, Jen...."

"Fuck!" said Jennifer, completely exasperated. "It didn't mean anything. Focus on the money, Rick." Then she turned to face me and waved the gun, almost daring me to say something else. The she pointed the weapon towards the black metal frame.

"Alright, mister funny man. Open it up."

I frowned at her. "What makes you think I know how?"

"You think I'm stupid. I'm not. You know what's in it and the only way you would is if you opened it. I don't know how you know how to open it but I don't care," She put the gun in my chest and I could see that it was a Sig Sauer, a Swiss/German weapon. Probably a P226. I happen to know a thing or two about guns. I've never had a Sig Sauer stuck in my chest before so that was new. "So open it."

I slowly moved to the flat file, turned the frame around and ran my hands along it until I got to the lock. The sun was on the back end of the house now but the gallery was still bright and well lit from outside. It had become a nice late afternoon, at least weather wise. Far off a dog barked and it sounded like the one I heard the first day I was here when I sat in the sunroom with Chandler. Seemed like a lifetime ago. It barked again and I thought *Run, Lassie! Get help!* but, unsurprisingly, that didn't work.

I dialed in 48, 49 and 50 and swung it open.

"Take it out," said Jennifer quietly. I could hear her breathing, slowly, her breath catching a bit. This was it, this was the big ticket for her. Sell these pages for God knows how much and stick it to her dad. Even though, the way this was going, I knew she and Rick didn't plan on dad feeling bad about it for long. They didn't plan on her father or Jessica or me feeling anything by the time they had their money. I thought about the X-acto blade in my pocket and just how I could do this without getting killed.

I took the Swan art out and moved it to the far end of the flat file top, next to the Romita Spider-man art. Then I lifted out the cover to *Fantastic Four* #48. Even in this tense, crazy situation I was still in awe of the King. We all were in awe but for different reasons. I put that down and then took out the cover to #49 and the splash to #50.

We all stared at them for a few seconds. Then, I heard Rick swallow and he said, "Like we talked about?"

Jennifer nodded and Rick herded me over to the far end of the room towards the south end of the house. He was sweating now and looked nervous, way more nervous than when I first came in.

This was it, then. They were going to shoot us and make

it look like I had some kind of beef with Chandler, probably over money, and then we pulled and shot each other. The gun Rick had was probably the same piece they used to kill Donnie's cousin and his boy. Put all the killings on me, nice and tidy. Any cop with brains could probably figure out that it was all set up, especially if they did a thorough forensics test but they were probably counting on it looking cut and dry. Some black guy smokes two well to do white people in their house but gets shot by one of them. Then Rick comes home and finds the bodies. It would probably work. I thought about Jennifer getting all of Chandler's money now anyway, if she killed him and Jessica. But she said she had been cut out of the will. Maybe this was her only way to get paid.

Rick was on my right and the knife was in my right pocket so I didn't know how I could reach it quickly without him noticing me. I didn't have any choice, though. As he watched Jennifer I slowly put my hand in and felt the cool, narrow handle. If I could stab him in the neck or face I could hurt him enough to get the gun away from him. Probably should go center mass and aim for the chest. Then once I had the gun I might have to shoot Jennifer. Jesus.

I was still a little too far from Rick too stab him cleanly. I was just about to slide closer when Chandler said, "Jennifer, this has gone far enough. Put that gun down!"

Jennifer looked at Chandler like he was insane and said "Dad, just be quiet." But Chandler took a step towards her.

"No. You're not getting this art, you're not going to threaten me and your sister in our home. Put the gun down."

Jennifer had casually been aiming in his direction but now she leveled the Sig at Chandler's chest. "Stop moving, dad, or I will shoot you."

As he shook off Jessica, who was trying to stop him, a look of amazement crossed Chandler's face. "You're going to shoot me? Your own father? No, you won't. Put. The gun. Down."

Rick said, "Shut up and stop fucking moving!" He was completely distracted and I knew this was my time. I gripped the handle of the blade in my pocket and started to pull it out. Once I got it out beyond the pocket I would have to step towards Rick and swing. Only had one shot at it.

"Dad, no!" said Jessica.

Jennifer took a step back but the gun didn't waver. "Dad!" she yelled. "Stop!"

I had the knife out and was looking at Rick when the shot went off.

It was deafening in that room with no carpet or soft chairs or soft anything to cushion the sound. The noise reverberated; stunning me for a second and when I looked

Chandler had a growing spot of blood on his chest. He looked at it and then Jennifer with a shocked expression on his face. He hadn't realized just how insane his daughter was until it was far too late. Chandler started to say something but nothing came out and he went down.

Jennifer took a step backwards, her eyes wide, her mouth a giant O. I don't think she could even believe that she had done it. When she turned to face Rick I was moving at him and swinging the blade. It caught him high in the chest up near his left shoulder and he screamed but didn't drop the gun. I pulled it out and saw Jennifer raising her gun towards me and thought for sure I was about to be shot until Jessica tackled her and the two went down in a pile.

Rick was bringing the Glock around towards me so I grabbed his right wrist and stabbed him in the forearm. This time, he dropped the gun but got me by my throat and shoved me. He was probably hoping to pin me against the wall but we sailed right out through the open door and into the hallway.

We both fell onto the hard wood floor, Rick on top. I lost the grip on the Xacto knife and it went flying. I heard it land a few feet away but it might as well had landed in China. Rick had me down good and was squeezing my throat even harder. I tried to roll him over but we were wedged against the wooden mahogany bannister, one of the upright balusters digging into my shoulder. I tried to throw him the other way but could get no leverage as he pinned me there. He was incredibly strong. I guess that shouldn't have come as a surprise.

I grabbed his thick arm and tried to push it up but it was like trying to push a fire hydrant. He tightened his grip on my neck and I fought for air. Then he raised his fist but I beat him to it and hit him with a left into his nose. He grunted and then, realizing he didn't have a clear shot at my face, drove a punch into my left side. It felt like I got hit with a swinging log. Everything got gray and there was a high-pitched whine in my ears and I knew in a few seconds I would be finished. I could see Rick gritting he teeth and blood running from his nose but it was like I was seeing it through a shower curtain. Through the haze I saw him raise his fist again and I swung at his nose as hard as I had ever swung before and heard a crunching, gristly sound as I connected.

Rick roared in pain, fell back off of me and grabbed his smashed nose. It was really bleeding now, a bright red stream flowing down into his mouth and Rick looked at his bloody hands in horror. It's a lot different when you're seeing your own blood, for a change. I scrambled to my feet and took in gulps of air. My ribs flared in pain but I forced myself at Rick, who was already up and coming at me.

He was heavier and stronger than me but I thought I had more momentum to push him back. We met in a rattling collision that made my side bark in agony and then I could feel myself falling backwards. He was just too strong. I looked to my right as we fell and I saw the curve of the bannister where it began its downward trek and realized that we were going down the stairs.

I threw my right hand out in desperation and caught a hold of one of the thick balusters. My back hit the stairs and something pulled in my right arm but I managed to keep my body from rolling over and held on. Rick sailed over me and down, smashing into the stairs and then up and over again until he came to rest at the landing below. I thought he may be dead but his screaming said otherwise.

I painfully pulled myself upright and looked down at Rick. He was staring at his left leg and I could see where the broken bone had punched through the skin about six inches up from the knee. Rick grabbed his leg with both hands and lay on his back, wailing. I figured he wasn't going anywhere for a while. I silently vowed to start working out again and painfully hustled back into the gallery.

When I came in I saw Jessica punch Jennifer in the mouth and then bend to pick up something. The flat file obscured whatever it was. Then I saw her rise and she was pointing the gun at Jennifer. Suddenly I had an irrational, crazy fear that somehow she was Jennifer, that she had in some terrible way changed clothes with her sister while I was fighting Rick. But it was a silly, scared thought that I knew wasn't true.

Jennifer got up and screamed something unintelligible at her sister. She was crying and her face was scratched and her hair was in a shock, shooting out in all directions. Jessica had really jacked her up. But Jennifer was too far gone to see that it was over. She screamed again and rushed at Jessica and Jessica shot her twice. The room shook with the sounds and Jennifer was pushed back until she crashed into a wall and down. An Eduardo Risso Batman page fell and hit the floor next to her body, glass scattering all around her head. Then it was quiet.

Jessica dropped the gun and knelt over her father. I came around the flat file, kicked the gun away from Jennifer and got down on the floor too. Chandler was still as Jessica took his hand but then his eyes fluttered open and his mouth moved like he wanted to say something. I couldn't believe he was still alive.

"Call 911," I told Jessica and she ran from the room. Jennifer and Rick had probably taken their cell phones away from them and put them in another room. Then Chandler groaned and blinked at me, like he was trying to focus on my face.

"Hold on, Mr. Chandler", I said, putting my hands over the chest wound, blood still rushing out. The entire front of his shirt was stained with it and more kept coming. There was so much. I didn't think that much blood could come out of somebody. I was shaking, trying to apply pressure like they say in the movies and my entire body from head to toe was shaking. "Tell me, uh… " I stammered. "Tell me more about Curt Swan. Anything."

Chandler looked up at me and for a crazy second I thought he was smiling and then another crazy second later I realized he was.

"I never…" he croaked, blood and spittle foaming on his lips. "I never even met the man."

And then he started to laugh, a choking, wheezing rasp of a laugh and before I knew it I was laughing too because it was kind of funny, even with all that had happened. Tears streamed from his eyes and I wasn't sure if it were from laughing or the pain or both. Then Jessica ran back in and knelt across from me, her eyes panicked.

"They're coming daddy!" she said and then looked confused at Chandler and me as we laughed. "Dad?" she asked shakily, gently touching his face.

Chandler stopped chuckling for a second, coughed and waved his hand feebly.

"I'm sorry, Jess… it's actually kind of…" he said and

then he coughed once more and just stopped. Everything going on in him just seemed to come to a halt and I knew he was dead.

A look of anguish came over Jessica's face and she bowed her head. She wept silently as I reached across Chandler's body and put my hand on her shoulder, trying somehow to be comforting. The loss of her mother and aunt had been, clearly, a terrible time for her. I couldn't even imagine what this was like.

I got up and went to check on Rick, taking the Sig with me. I had half a mind to shoot him but he was where I had left him before, on his back and writhing in pain at the bottom of the stairs. He had managed to take off his shirt and make a tourniquet of it, staunching the flow of blood from his damaged leg. He saw me and started yelling but I just mentally drowned him out. Then I walked down past him and down the next flight to wait for the police.

17

To say that the rest of that day went by in a blur would imply that it went by rapidly. It did not. It crawled and limped on in surreal fashion and I felt like I was the lead in an extremely long play, a play with a very tragic ending. Very Shakespearean. There was no miracle happy ending, no last minute heroics to save the day. No *Deus ex machina* here, sorry.

I answered the front door and let the first pair of cops that showed up see my hands very clearly. I made no sudden moves or strange, peculiar motions. Think what you want but reports of a shooting in a rather nice neighborhood can have dire consequences for a black man, especially one covered in blood. So I played Mr. Good Citizen and pointed to the gun that I had put down in the living room and stayed as far away from it as possible. I ain't trying to get dead.

While I was giving the cops a brief rundown, Rick, who was still sitting by the steps on the second floor with his busted leg, tried to throw me under the bus and claim I was the shooter and the guy who tossed him, the innocent in all of this, down the stairs. There was a split second of tension until Jessica came down and set the cops straight. Thank God she was there. I briefly entertained the notion of "accidentally" stepping on Rick's leg but thought better of it.

A bunch of EMS people showed up and after I buzzed them in they got a brief update on the casualties from the cops. A couple stopped to take care of Rick and a few more hurried upstairs. I didn't think they had anything to rush for but when I got up there they were working on Jennifer, who was still alive, They had already pronounced Chandler and Jessica sat quietly looking at his body. She didn't even concern herself with her sister. She might as well been dead.

More cops arrived. A lot more. I guess they had stationed a uniform by the open gate outside because pretty soon the house looked like a police academy graduation. They seemed to be everywhere. I'm sure stuff like this didn't happen often in this part of South Orange so a murder here was a big deal. Luckily for them it was already solved. The first two cops officially took my statement and another set took Jessica into another room and spoke to her.

Soon after two detectives came in and after talking with the uniforms, zeroed in on me. Their names were Gallo and Moreland, Gallo being older with shifty eyes and Moreland being a big, rosy-cheeked guy in a suit that was too small for him. He looked like he had played football at Columbia High down the street and just fell into police work. On the contrary, Gallo looked like he was born wearing a badge. I thought about Tidyman and Himes and having to eventually deal with them and not really looking forward to it.

By then I felt even more like I was in a dream, a truly bad dream that just wouldn't end. I was exhausted. I guess the adrenaline flow was gone and now I was just smoked, mentally and physically. The made me tell my story three times and I guess I told it the same way every time, even though I was distracted by EMS taking Jennifer out on a stretcher and Chandler in a body bag. Jessica followed them out and our eyes met briefly as she passed. She looked so beaten and tired, so worn away by everything. My heart just broke looking at her and I wanted to comfort her but this wasn't the time or place. She mouthed "I'll call you later", gave me a little wave and then she was gone.

I didn't want to be in this house anymore. I wanted to be anywhere else, doing anything else, just trying to get past this crazy nightmare. But they kept asking me questions and pretty soon the two detectives and I piled into a car and went to a police station, where I got to answer more questions for what seemed like forever. Maybe wanting to get out of the house wasn't such a good idea.

They asked me if I wanted a lawyer and I said I didn't need one, which in hindsight was very dumb. But I didn't have a lawyer and I just wanted to go home. I didn't want to deal with lawyers and cops and police stations anymore. I just took it. It all seemed like a movie, like this was something that was being performed for me. Then, because I clearly wasn't having enough fun, an angry Tidyman and Himes came in and threw words and phrases at me like "obstruction" and "conspiracy" and "withholding evidence". Right after that, a man who I had never seen before in my life came in and said that his name was Morris Lieberman and that he represented me and Jessica Chandler and he proceeded to throw words and phrases back at Tidyman and Himes and the South Orange cops, stuff I have never heard before. But they must've been damned good words because it just completely chilled everybody out. Lieberman picked me up by my elbow and as we were heading out Tidyman scowled at me and said something like

"Don't even think about taking a trip, Farrar." *Madison! Don't leave town!* I just nodded tiredly and Lieberman shot Tidyman a death stare and soon we were standing on the front steps of the precinct house, with me suddenly realizing that it was night. An unusually warm night, too. It would've been a great night if people weren't dead and lives weren't ruined. But I guess you could say that about any night.

Lieberman looked over at me and said, "You ok?"

"Yeah. Just… " I shook my head and rubbed my eyes with the heels of my hands. I felt as tired as I had ever felt in my entire life. "Long day."

Lieberman nodded. "Longer still for Jessica. She's at the hospital with her sister. The doctors don't expect her to make it."

"Jesus."

Lieberman sighed. "I had been Chandler's lawyer for twelve years. My father was for twenty-two years before that. This was not exactly the ending for him that I expected."

I nodded. "I can imagine."

We stood there silently for a few more seconds and then Lieberman started down the steps. "Come on. I'll give you a lift back to your car."

While we were heading over to the house in Lieberman's Beemer I said, "I didn't thank you. Those guys were climbing all over me."

Lieberman smiled. "They have absolutely nothing on you. Nothing. They got the killers and the motive and the means and everything else. They can't hang anything on you."

"I never had a lawyer before. How do we go about..."

"I am on permanent retainer to the Chandler family," Then he caught himself. "To Jessica Chandler. It's all taken care of."

"Thank you." I said again. I didn't know what else to say.

"Least we could do. She'll get in touch when she has a chance. Not sure when that will be, though."

"I understand."

When we reached a red light he pulled a business card out of his suit jacket and handed it to me. "When those Brooklyn cops or these South Orange ones get in touch with you call me. Do not see them without me. Alright?"

"Thank you, " I said again and put the card in my wallet. I had a lawyer. It was nice and all but I wished the events that had led to me having one never occurred.

We drove up North Ridgewood Road and turned into the drive of the house. Across the street were a few news vans and there were a couple of reporters doing stand ups.

Everyone reacted to us arriving and the lights turned to face us, the cameramen scrambling to get a good shot. I looked away.

We went through the open gate and past the squad car that was sitting off to the side and up the drive. There were still cops about and some regular people, maybe friends of the family or something. But the house looked different to me and not just because I had never seen it at night. It looked empty and foreboding like something in a ghost story. Haunted. Maybe it was just me that was haunted.

After we pulled up next to my Jeep, Lieberman said, "Go home. Drink a beer or a shot or whatever and try to get some rest. Ok?"

I nodded, shook his hand and opened the car door. "I'll try."

"Ok. And don't hesitate to call me. I am your legal counsel. You let me know of anything the cops do or say. Alright?"

I got out of the car and stretched my back. Every part of me felt achy, including my arm and my side, which felt even more so. "I will."

"Good. Go home, Will."

"Definitely." I said and fished out my car keys. Lieberman waved, turned the BMW around and was gone down the drive.

I got in the Jeep and took a deep breath. Then I looked at the house again. There were still lights on up in the gallery and I could see people milling about. Then a flash from a camera. Crime scene. I closed my eyes and saw Chandler with that look of absolute shock on his face and a growing splotch of red on his shirt. I shook my head to push it out.

There was another burst of light from the gallery. I watched people move around in the room for a few more minutes and then I started up the Jeep and drove home.

It was yet another terrible night of sleep. I woke up about six times during the night and each time I thought for sure that the whole thing had been a dream. But then I would lay there in the dark and think and feel the soreness in my body and know that it really did happen. No *Dallas* TV show fake out, no Patrick Duffy in the shower. Which was good because I really did not want to see Patrick Duffy in my shower. Finally, I rolled out of bed at 9:17, staggered into the kitchen for a Pepsi and plopped down on the couch.

After I turned on SportsCenter and became vaguely aware that last night had become a typical night in New York sports (Knicks, Mets lose, Yankees stage miracle comeback at the Stadium) I just kind of sat there and rubbed

Thor's neck and back while she purred happily. I was completely lost in thought when my phone rang. I answered it without seeing who it was and was momentarily startled by the soft voice on the other end.

"Hi, William. It's Jessica."

I sat upright on the couch and stopped rubbing Thor, who looked at me like a queen might look at one of her disobedient servants.

"Hey. How are you? I mean, are you ok?"

"Hanging in. Tired. Really tired."

"I bet," I said. "How's Jennifer?"

She paused for a bit and I knew the answer before she even said it. "Jennifer died about six o'clock this morning."

"I'm sorry," I said, which seemed weird in a way. But Jennifer was still blood to her and a twin. Despite what she had done there was still that.

"Thank you," Jessica said quietly.

"If there is anything I can do…" I said, not really knowing what I could do for her. The girl was loaded now. Why would she need me?

"Actually, there is something," she said, surprising me. "I want to sell my father's art collection. And I want you to arrange it."

That stunned me into silence for a few seconds. Then I said, "Jessica. Are you sure? I mean, there's a lifetime of comic art collecting in there."

"That was dad's passion," she said. "I don't really know anything about it. And with him gone it's just a room with art in it. I want to sell those pieces and donate the money to some charities. I don't need it. And I know you love comic art as much as dad and will do a great job of moving it. At a commission, of course."

"Wow," I said. "Ok. I guess. If that's what you really want."

"It is. But one thing. I want you to take the Superman cover and the Fantastic Four art. Sell it or keep it, whatever. I want that to be yours."

I was speechless for a few seconds.

"No," I finally said. "I can't. Do you know how much money that's worth?" Then I realized how silly I sounded saying that to a girl that just tragically walked into more money than I would ever see in my life. "Do you know how much that could bring to a charity?"

"Yes. I think it would do wonders for the William Farrar Charity. Listen, I've already decided. And I know my father would approve. He was so impressed with your knowledge and love of the art. So this isn't me asking. It's me telling you."

I realized that arguing was a waste of time so I just gave up. "Thank you."

"Well, don't thank me yet," she said. "That art is evidence. So you'll have to wait until after Rick's trial, be it three months or six months or whatever. And then it's yours."

"I can wait. I've lived all this time without it already. What's six more months?"

She laughed and said "Good attitude," and then we were both quiet for a few seconds. Then she said, "So… you really thought she was me?"

I felt embarrassed and said, "Come on. You guys look just alike."

"Well…" said Jessica and I could hear a tone just like I had heard from her sister when she was in my apartment. "I'll have you know that I do everything better than Jennifer."

"Wow." I said and chuckled. These Chandler girls were certainly a flirty duo.

She laughed again and said, "Sorry. Just dealing with it all… you know?"

"I do. I mean, what you've gone through is pretty extreme but… I do know."

There was another pause and she said, "Listen. Maybe when the dust settles a bit we can get together... to talk about selling the art? Over coffee?"

"I would like that."

"Ok, then," she said. I could hear a little smile on her end. I was glad she had one because smiles would be few and far between in the next few days. Probably longer. "I will be in touch, Mr. Farrar."

"Look forward to it, Ms. Chandler. And take care. If you want to talk at any time just call."

She said she would and hung up and I sat there, a lot more awake and aware then I was before she called. I thought about the four pieces of art that would one day come my way. I would sell the Fantastic Four pages. Yes, it was Kirby and a landmark moment in Marvel history but it was also worth so much. That money would change my life. I would try to sell all three to one buyer. I might even use an auction house. Nah.... I would do it myself. I knew enough people who knew enough people. And those people would kill to have Silver Age King Kirby artwork. I sadly knew that for a fact, already.

The Superman cover? That I would keep. Its value would skyrocket after this story came out. People would flock to own it and have the Swan cover that was the face of a crazy murder mystery. But no, I won't sell it. Whether I still live here or someplace else I would keep it in that crazy custom black frame with the same combination and hang it right in the middle of my collection to remember Coleman Chandler by. Not the Coleman Chandler that lied to me and used the Swan piece as a front. I would keep it to remember the Coleman Chandler who collected comic art in his own gallery and proudly showed it to me one day because he was happy to meet someone who loved it as much as he did.

It was the least I could do.

ABOUT THE AUTHOR

Kevin Greene was born and raised in Brooklyn, New York and, showing an attribute for art, went to the High School of Art and Design and the School Of Visual Arts, both in Manhattan. He has worked in the art field as a freelance artist and caricaturist and in the apparel industry as a graphic designer. This is his first novel. In 2012 he published an art book called Heroes and Villains: The Science Fiction Caricature Art of Kevin Greene, which combines his love of Sci-Fi movies and television with his love of caricature. It is available to purchase on Amazon, Alibris.com and iTunes.

He currently lives in South Orange, New Jersey.